SPEEDWAY PUBLIC LIBRARY

3 5550 42986 3577

P9-DZP-100

DEW DROP DEAD

J   HOW
Howe, James
Dew drop dead

WITHDRAWN
Speedway Public Library

$t/95$

SPEEDWAY PUBLIC LIBRARY
SPEEDWAY, INDIANA

Other **SEBASTIAN BARTH** *Mysteries by*
James Howe

EAT YOUR POISON, DEAR • STAGE FRIGHT • WHAT ERIC KNEW

Avon Camelot Books

THE CELERY STALKS AT MIDNIGHT • CREEPY-CRAWLY BIRTHDAY
THE FRIGHT BEFORE CHRISTMAS • HOT FUDGE
HOWLIDAY INN • MORGAN'S ZOO
NIGHTY-NIGHTMARE • PINKY AND REX
PINKY AND REX GET MARRIED • PINKY AND REX AND THE SPELLING BEE
PINKY AND REX AND THE MEAN OLD WITCH • PINKY AND REX GO TO CAMP
SCARED SILLY

Avon Flare Books

A NIGHT WITHOUT STARS

Avon Camelot Books by
Deborah and James Howe

BUNNICULA: A RABBIT-TALE OF MYSTERY

JAMES HOWE is the author of numerous books for children, including the popular series about Bunnicula, the vampire rabbit, and his friends, Harold, Chester, and Howie. Among his books are *Morgan's Zoo, A Night Without Stars,* and the other Sebastian Barth mysteries: *Stage Fright, Eat Your Poison, Dear,* and *What Eric Knew.* The author lives in Hastings-on-Hudson, New York, with his wife, Betsy Imershein, and their daughter, Zoe.

Avon Books are available at special quantity discounts for bulk purchases for sales promotions, premiums, fund raising or educational use. Special books, or book excerpts, can also be created to fit specific needs.

For details write or telephone the office of the Director of Special Markets, Avon Books, Dept. FP, 1350 Avenue of the Americas, New York, NY 10019, 1-800-238-0658.

DEW DROP DEAD

JAMES HOWE

AN AVON CAMELOT BOOK

If you purchased this book without a cover, you should be aware that
this book is stolen property. It was reported as "unsold and destroyed"
to the publisher, and neither the author nor the publisher has received
any payment for this "stripped book."

AVON BOOKS
A division of
The Hearst Corporation
1350 Avenue of the Americas
New York, New York 10019

"A Jean Karl book"
Copyright © 1990 by James Howe
Published by arrangement with Atheneum Publishers, an imprint of Macmillan
Publishing Company
Library of Congress Catalog Card Number: 89-34697
ISBN: 0-380-71301-2
RL: 4.9

All rights reserved, which includes the right to reproduce this book or portions
thereof in any form whatsoever except as provided by the U.S. Copyright Law.
For information address Atheneum Publishers, Macmillan Publishing Company,
866 Third Avenue, New York, New York 10022.

First Avon Camelot Printing: September 1991

CAMELOT TRADEMARK REG. U.S. PAT. OFF. AND IN OTHER COUNTRIES, MARCA REG-
ISTRADA, HECHO EN U.S.A.

Printed in the U.S.A.

OPM 10 9 8 7 6

To Betsy—
for her love, her encouragement,
and her paper clips

SPEEDWAY PUBLIC LIBRARY
SPEEDWAY, INDIANA

1

Sebastian Barth sat listening to his parents argue. His hand rested on a piece of paper, blank but for the words *Dear Koji*. He'd hoped that writing a letter to his pen pal in Japan would distract him from the fighting; unfortunately, it seemed to be working the other way around. Each time he thought of something to write, angry words flew up through the floorboards of his room and buzzed his brain like a swarm of attacking bees.

"I don't *want* to move any more than you do," he heard his father say.

"What makes you think *your* work is all that matters?"

"I'm not saying that."

"Well, what *are* you saying?"

"Come on, Katie—"

"Don't take that patient tone with me, William Barth. It's condescending and you know it."

"For crying out loud—"

Dear Koji, How's everything with you? I'm having a pretty good year in school. Mom and Dad are fine. Gram is busy with all her projects, as usual. There's not much happening here.

Lies, Sebastian thought. Why don't you just write the truth? Dear Koji, Guess what? I lost my radio show and it looks like Dad's about to lose his job. We might even have to move because there aren't many radio stations around here where he can find work. Mom's having a fit because she doesn't want to leave her restaurant. Even Gram is depressed.

How's the weather there? It's been really cold here. We've had snow and it isn't even Thanksgiving yet. I think we're in for a rough winter—

"You're not listening to me, Will!"

"I'm listening, I'm listening. I'm just not hearing anything!"

Well, at least that part's true, Sebastian thought. We're definitely in for a rough winter.

A door slammed. A second door slammed. All he heard now was the murmuring of his grandmother's reasonable tones. He wasn't sure who was left for her to be talking to; he imagined it was one of the cats.

He looked out his window at the house across the street. There was a car in the driveway. Good, he thought, they're back. Sebastian shoved his feet into his sneakers and charged down the stairs. Before his grandmother could ask where he was going, he grabbed a jacket and was out the door.

It was three-thirty. There was still time to salvage what had thus far been a thoroughly rotten Saturday.

2

"David's in the bathroom and my father's having a crisis and I'm helping," said Rachel Lepinsky as she opened the door. Rachel was the nine-year-old sister of Sebastian's best friend. She turned away, then said, "Wait. As long as you're here, what do you think of this title?" Consulting a notebook, she read, *"The Case of the Mysterious Thing."*

"Catchy," said Sebastian. "What's it about?"

"I don't know. I'm just coming up with titles. It's my dad's job to write the stupid books."

"Oh. Well, that sounds like a perfect title for a stupid book."

Rachel glared at Sebastian and left the room. A moment later, he heard her voice coming from down the hall near her father's office. She was reading him her title. Then he heard Josh.

"Please, Rachel, I appreciate your desire to help. But all I want right now is to be left alone. Close the door on your way out."

By the time Rachel came back into the living room, she was no longer carrying her notebook. "I have decided that writing is a pointless profession," she said. "It makes you cranky and not fun to be with. Besides, all you do all day is sit in a room by yourself and make up stories. It's not very down-to-

3

earth, if you ask me. Whatever I do when I grow up, it will be down-to-earth, that's for sure."

"Hey, Rachel, I've got the perfect profession for you," David Lepinsky shouted as he came down the stairs. "It's down-to-earth, and you never have to be by yourself."

"What?"

"Mud wrestling."

"Very *un*funny," Rachel said. She fell back into a chair and crossed her arms.

"Let's go somewhere," David said to Sebastian. "It's bad news around here today." To Rachel, he said, "Tell Dad I went out."

"Sure," Rachel said. "I'll tell him you ran away to join the circus."

"Do that."

"Boy," said Sebastian once they were outside, "I thought things were grim around *my* house. What's going on?"

"It's my dad," David said. "He's got writer's block. We went to the mall for clothes and all he could talk about were story ideas. See, he's owed his editor a book for almost a year now and he's stuck. Last night, he had this dream that the publishing company came and took away his word processor."

"Wow."

"And today while Rachel was trying on shoes, he got this idea for a mystery where the murderer is a shoe salesman who kills people by cutting off their circulation at the ankles. The worst part was that he was serious. That's when we came home."

"I've never seen him like this."

"Yeah, it's pretty bad. What's happening at your

house? Does it still look like your father's going to get fired?"

The boys were leaning against the railing on David's front porch. Sebastian said, "It doesn't look good."

They fell silent, as they always did at this point in this particular conversation. They had been friends for as far back as they could remember and they did not want to consider the possibility that Sebastian might have to move away.

"It's too cold to hang around," Sebastian said. "Let's go for a ride. I'll get my bike and meet you."

"Where to?"

"Anywhere. Who knows? Maybe we'll find a circus to join."

3

Corrie Wingate waved to them from the front lawn of her house down the street. "Where are you going?" she called out.

Sebastian and David brought their bikes to a halt by the curb.

"To find a circus," David said. He knew she was going to end up joining them, but he couldn't quite bring himself to invite her. Corrie had moved into the neighborhood the summer before, and it had taken David some time to warm up to her. By now he was used to the idea that she was Sebastian's girlfriend. He didn't like it, but he was used to it.

And Corrie was used to the fact that David rarely gave a straight answer. "Can I come, too?" she said.

"Sure," said Sebastian.

Corrie ran to get her bicycle, which was propped against a tree. "I've got to get away from my house for a while," she told them. "My father is driving me nuts."

"Welcome to the club," Sebastian said.

"*Your* father?" David was incredulous. Corrie's father was a minister. He didn't think ministers were allowed to drive you nuts.

"Please," said Corrie. "All he can talk about is how his 'flock' is letting him down. He's been trying to start this food-and-shelter program at the church, and now that he's gotten an official go-ahead, he can't get enough volunteers. He says people are too selfish these days, that they don't think of others. *Me,* he's telling. Me, who spent two hours this morning delivering meals to shut-ins. I mean, if he wants to talk about my brother Drew, maybe. My sister, Alice, for sure. But me? It's gotten to the point where every time he starts in about his flock, I just go, 'Baa-aa-aa.' "

Sebastian laughed.

"You know what he said?" Corrie went on. "He said he wished he was back in Troy. Can you believe it? He'd rather be in Troy, New York, than Pembroke, Connecticut. He said the problems there were more real, whatever that means."

"Pembroke has real problems," Sebastian said.

"I know that. And so does he. I think he just likes to hear himself complain."

"Grown-ups," said David. "I'm glad I'm not one."

"You will be soon enough," Sebastian reminded him.

"I don't know," said David. "Maybe I'll stay twelve the rest of my life."

"I thought the same thing when I was your age," Sebastian said. "And then one day, you know what? I turned thirteen."

"Aw, you're such an old man," said David.

"Yeah? I'll bet I can still beat you to the traffic light."

"Bet you can't."

"You're on."

Sebastian and David sped away without a backward glance. Corrie noticed that she hadn't been in-

7

cluded in their little bet, but she didn't let it bother her. She watched them pedal furiously down Chestnut Street, Sebastian leading by a hair, then pushed off at her own leisurely pace. After a moment, she picked up her speed.

It was a close race. By the time the boys arrived at the traffic light, they were neck and neck. Fortunately, Corrie was already there to call the winner.

4

Heading out Route 7, they slowed their pace and got to talking about Sebastian's canceled radio show. For three years, he had been the host of "Small Talk," a weekly talk show for kids. The opportunity had come his way because his father was the station manager of WEB-FM; it had never occurred to him that he could be fired.

"I knew the ratings were slipping," he told David and Corrie as they passed the A&P, "but it still came as a shock. I mean, do you know what it's like to have your own dad give you the boot?"

David, who wrote for Sebastian's show, had been with him that day. "It was awful," he told Corrie. "We came in to tape the show, and Uncle Will said, 'Boys, I have some bad news.'"

"It wasn't his fault. It was Herself," said Sebastian, referring to the anonymous and eccentric station owner. "She sent out this memo. She says nobody listens to talk radio anymore. So what does she do? She puts on this music like you hear in elevators. Gee, that'll get a lot of new listeners. Not that I think she cares much anyway. The rumor is she's planning to sell the station to some big corporation. What gets me is that I never had the chance to quit. I wish my father would."

9

"Quit?" David asked.

"Yeah, just so he won't have to get fired."

"Don't say that, Sebastian," said Corrie.

"But it feels lousy to get fired. I know. I'm thirteen and a has-been."

David laughed. "There you go sounding like an old man again."

"I know, I know. I've got my whole life ahead of me and all that. But what about my dad? He's thirty-seven. What's he going to do?"

No one answered. They had reached the top of Dead Man's Hill and were silenced, as always, by the prospect of what lay before them. The steep decline with its hairpin turns was a favorite for daredevil coasting among the kids in town.

"Want to turn around?" Corrie asked.

That was all David needed to hear. "What's the matter?" he said. "Afraid?"

"No," Corrie said. "But it'll be dark soon. We don't want to get too far from home."

"It's not so late. What do you say, Sebastian?"

"I say let's go for it."

"All right!"

Sebastian felt the raw November wind sting his cheeks. His eyes were beginning to water. "Let's take a right at the bottom," he suggested. "We'll go as far as the inn and then head back."

Corrie asked, "What inn?"

"It's called the Dew Drop Inn," said Sebastian. "It's about a half-mile up Sunflower. If you get there before us—" He stopped himself and smiled at Corrie. "I guess I should say, *since* you'll get there before us, wait up. I think there's a sign out front."

Corrie smiled back. "I can't help it if I happen to

10

be in great shape," she said. "Anyway, why wouldn't there be a sign?"

"The place closed about a year ago. It's all boarded up now."

"The owners disappeared," said David. Then he added, with an eyebrow raised for emphasis, "Mysteriously."

"*The Mystery of the Boarded-Up Windows*," said Corrie.

"I'll have to tell my father that one," David said. "It beats *The Mystery of the Strangled Ankles*, anyway."

"First," said Sebastian, zipping his jacket to help cut the wind, "we have the mystery of Dead Man's Hill. Will we survive? Or will an eighteen-wheeler turn us into ghosts doomed to ride our bikes across the midnight sky through all eternity?"

"Oo-oo-oo," David moaned.

Sebastian said, "On your marks, get set—"

"Go!" Corrie screamed. And she screamed all the way down.

5

Corrie picked up so much speed going down Dead Man's Hill, she barely had to pedal once she hit Sunflower Road. She was still out of breath when she caught sight of the impressive white building looming up on her right. There was a hand-painted sign by the road's edge, but the chain had rusted so badly over the previous winter that one end had broken loose, leaving the wooden board to dangle awkwardly and noisily in the wind. Corrie tried to ignore its plaintive crying as she waited for her friends at the end of the circular driveway.

At close range, the place looked the way the sign sounded: forlorn. What had once been a magnificent roadhouse with stately pillars and black shutters at every window was now a mess of peeling paint and plywood patches. It was hard for Corrie to believe it had been inhabited as short a time as a year ago.

Sebastian and David arrived only a minute or two after Corrie, but it felt to her as if a much longer time had passed. She'd forgotten all about Dead Man's Hill; what she wanted to know was the story of Dew Drop Inn.

"I don't know a lot about it," Sebastian said as they walked their bikes up the gravel driveway. Weeds were everywhere. "I'm sure Gram could tell us its history." Sebastian's grandmother was on the board of the local historical society.

"Mrs. Hallem knows *everything* about Pembroke," David said.

"Not everything," said Sebastian. "She doesn't know what happened to the people who owned it."

"But how did it get like this so fast?" Corrie asked. "It's sad, don't you think?"

They had let their bicycles drop onto the overgrown lawn and were walking around the side of the property.

David shrugged. "It's only a building," he said.

"It's more than a building," said Corrie, "it's a piece of history. I'll bet it's from Colonial times. You have no social conscience, David."

Before David could respond, Sebastian said, "Hey, look, one of the windows is open."

"Which one?"

"There, in the back," Sebastian pointed. The plywood planks on one of the first-floor windows had been yanked loose, the window itself jimmied open.

"Do you suppose somebody broke in?" Corrie asked.

"No, the squirrels did it," David said. He was going to add something about "dumb girls" when it occurred to him that Corrie would cream him if he did.

"You know what I mean," Corrie said. "Maybe the place has been robbed."

"Or maybe somebody's living here," said Sebastian.

Corrie raised her eyebrows. "Do you think so?"

"There's one way to find out."

"Sebastian," David said, "are you suggesting we go in there? I mean, I know you like a good mystery and all, but we could be asking for trouble."

"If Eric were here, we'd do it," Sebastian said, referring to a friend who had moved away the previous summer. Eric had led Sebastian and David on

13

many adventures, most of which had gotten them into trouble sooner or later.

"I think we should go home," Corrie said.

"Me, too," said David, surprised to find he was agreeing with Corrie.

Sebastian looked at Corrie, then David. "I don't believe you two," he said. "You want to go home. Half an hour ago, you couldn't wait to get away. We said we were looking for a circus, didn't we? Well, this is even better."

"I hate to point this out, Sebastian," said David, "but what we'd be doing is against the law. Breaking and entering is a crime, you know."

"We wouldn't be breaking, only entering."

"But it isn't right," Corrie argued. "I mean, even if it weren't illegal, it's not our property."

Sebastian sighed. "You said I like a good mystery. Well, this is a *great* mystery. Who opened the window? Why did they do it? Maybe there *was* a robbery. Just think, if we find evidence of a real crime, we'll be helping the police."

"We could help the police by letting them know about the window," said Corrie. "We don't have to go *in*. Besides, it'll be dark in there. We won't be able to see anything."

"No sweat," Sebastian retorted. "I have a flashlight in my bike bag. What do you say?" Corrie and David looked at each other.

"Well," said David, "it'll be better than listening to my father try to come up with ideas for a book. Hey, maybe this will give us one."

"Right," Sebastian said as he ran to get his flashlight. *"The Case of the Invaded Inn."*

14

"The Inn-Vasion!" David shouted.

"Dew Drop Inn," Corrie said to herself. Then she called out, "Hey, I've got one: *Dew Drop Dead!*"

They all laughed.

6

The beam from Sebastian's flashlight stole over the sheet-covered furniture like a cat on the prowl. "Ghosts," Corrie whispered, referring to the sheets. David said nothing, but sucked in his breath to keep from giggling, which he tended to do when he was nervous. Right now, he was very nervous.

The window they had climbed through had brought them into a large, informal dining room. From there they had passed into what appeared to be a sitting room. An oil painting of ducks in flight— not a very good one—graced the wall over the mantel. The stone fireplace was huge, taller than David, about even with Sebastian if he stood half-up on tiptoes. The mantel was covered with a layer of dust, knickknacks, and framed photographs.

"I wonder who those people are," Corrie said, referring to the latter. Her voice was hushed but no longer a whisper. She was gathering courage.

"It looks like they were taken a long time ago," Sebastian said.

"The nineteen fifties," said David. "I recognize the clothes."

With his flashlight, Sebastian spotlighted a faded black-and-white photograph of a smiling couple posed with their two children in front of a sailboat.

The younger child, a boy, wore glasses in heavy plastic frames and a strange-looking fur hat with a tail.

"What a goofus," said David.

"I think he's sweet," Corrie said. She squinted to make out the name on the side of the boat. *"Happy Times,"* she read. "Gee, don't you wonder what happens to people?"

"Maybe they're under here!" David shouted. He yanked a sheet off a chair with a loud whoop that made Corrie scream and Sebastian drop his flashlight.

"David!" Corrie cried.

"Nice move," said Sebastian, picking up the light. He shook it to make sure it worked. It did, but only intermittently.

"Sorry," David said, "I couldn't help myself. It was getting too serious in here." Then, to make amends, he asked, "Any signs of a robbery, Sherlock?" Sebastian was playing the beam of light around the room.

"Not that I can see. It's weird, though, isn't it?"

"What?" Corrie asked.

"The way there are still pictures on the fireplace, and look, there's even a magazine lying open on the floor by that chair. It's as if the people who were living here, or staying here, or whatever, just picked up and left."

"Maybe you were right," said David. "Maybe someone's living here now."

Sebastian knelt down to take a look at the magazine. "Detective stories," he said with a laugh.

"Listen," Corrie said, "if someone *is* living here, they could be watching us or listening. How do we

17

know they're not going to jump out with an ax or something?"

"We don't," said David. "Heh, heh, heh."

"You're a riot," Corrie said.

The light went out and Sebastian shook the flashlight to bring it back. "Special effects by David Lepinsky," he said. "Let's see what's in that room."

They moved through an open door into a spacious entrance hallway. "Wow," Corrie said. To their right was a tall grandfather clock stopped at twelve-o-five. Above them was a delicate chandelier with lighting fixtures meant to look like candles. And to their left a majestic staircase wound its way to the second floor.

"Well, at least the clock isn't ticking," David said. "And there isn't blood dripping off the chandelier."

"David, stop it," said Corrie, crossing to the grandfather clock and touching it gently. "It's beautiful, isn't it? I love this kind of clock, with the moon and the sun on its face. If anyone were going to commit a robbery, this is what they would take. Do you have any idea how valuable this is?"

"And so easy to get out of a window," David said. He could not see Corrie glare at him in the darkness that suddenly engulfed them when the light went out again.

Sebastian gave the flashlight a shake and said, "Let's go upstairs."

"What?" David said. "Tell the truth, Sebastian. Now that you're no longer a radio celebrity, are you hoping to make news as a famous murder victim? I say, let's get out of here while we still have all our body parts." He looked to Corrie for her support. He didn't find it.

18

"This place is amazing," she said, her eyes following the path of the staircase. "I mean, it's scary and all. But it's neat, too. I'm dying to find out what's up there."

David sighed. "I'll try not to take that literally," he said.

"You can wait down here, chicken heart," said Sebastian.

"No, thanks. If you and Corrie are going to get murdered, I wouldn't want to miss the fun."

"Let's go then."

As they made their way up the stairs, their fears grew with each step. David was so nervous he forgot to worry about giggling, although the inside of his cheek hurt from where he was biting it.

When they reached the top, they found themselves in the middle of a long hallway. Sebastian swept his light to the left, then to the right. All the bedroom doors but one were closed. No one spoke, even when Sebastian set off in the direction of the open door.

The darkness wrapped itself around them as they followed the flickering light down the carpeted hall. Sebastian muttered, "Don't fail me, light. Come on, don't go out. That's it, just a few more steps."

By the time they'd covered half the distance between the stairs and the open doorway, they were in the grip of a terror so real they had all begun to wonder what had possessed them to enter that open window. It was as if they had passed into another dimension, one in which time had stopped as surely as it had on the face of the grandfather clock downstairs. They were a million miles from their homes, their families, their real lives. They were in a dream.

A few feet from the door, a thought came to Sebastian. It was something he'd seen, something that hadn't registered—until now. The magazine he'd looked at in the sitting room had been dated. It was this month's issue.

There was a good chance they were not alone.

Sebastian almost turned back when he realized he was standing in the open doorway and his light was shining through. David and Corrie huddled close to him, shivering, they told themselves, because they were cold. The sight of the room, its commonplace and seemingly untouched furniture, came as such a relief it made them laugh. David laughed so hard he got the hiccoughs, and that made them laugh all the harder. Corrie begged them to stop because she had to go to the bathroom. The beam of light bounced off the objects in the room as Sebastian's hand jiggled and shook. Then it caught something. And their laughter died.

There was a body on the bed.

7

The sound of the flashlight hitting the hardwood floor was lost in their screams. They wanted to run, but held themselves in place for the eternity it took Sebastian to kneel down and grope in the darkness. He felt something and jumped. When he realized that what he'd touched wasn't flesh but metal, he grabbed it. The light flickered. It worked.

Sebastian raised the beam for the briefest moment. The body on the bed hadn't moved.

David hiccoughed loudly.

The sound was like a starter's gun. They scrambled away, tripping and clutching clumsily at each other as if they were running a sack race. The whole way down the stairs, through the entrance hallway, the sitting room, the dining room, and out the window, the only thing they heard was David's hiccoughing and occasional fits of giggling. Their hearts beat a wild tom-tom: Let me out, let me out, let me out.

Once they were out, they didn't stop to notice that it was almost dark. They didn't even stop to catch their breaths until they'd reached the end of Sunflower Road and Dead Man's Hill rose up before them like a wall.

"What do we do now?" David asked, his heavy

21

breathing only aggravating the hiccoughs that shook his thin body.

"Go home," Corrie said.

"Go to the police," said Sebastian.

"Let's go home first," Corrie said. *"Please."*

"Oh, right. You needed to go to the bathroom."

Corrie felt her cheeks burn. "Too late for that," she said.

"You peed in your pants?" David cried, sounding younger than twelve. "Corrie peed in her pants. Corrie peed in her pants."

"Oh, shut up, David," said Corrie. "I wouldn't talk if I were you. You giggle like a monkey."

"Would you two cut it out?" Sebastian said. "We've got more important things to deal with than who peed in their pants and who giggles like a monkey. Like a dead body. We've got to tell the police right away."

"I don't think whoever is in that bed is going anywhere in a hurry," David pointed out. "And maybe we shouldn't tell the police. Let's not forget we were breaking the law ourselves. Maybe we should call them. You know, an anonymous tip."

"Murder and going through an open window aren't exactly in the same league as far as breaking the law. Besides, Alex is our friend."

David nodded. He knew that Police Chief Alex Theopoulos might not be pleased about what they'd done, but David also knew he'd probably let them off with a wag of his finger and a wink of his eye. Especially in light of what they'd discovered.

"Don't you think we should get going?" said Corrie. "It's a long way up, and it's getting dark."

As they made their slow and painful journey up

22

Dead Man's Hill, their breathlessness made it impossible to speak. But their minds were filled with the one thought they would have spoken if they could:

We have seen death.

8

"Whoa, slow down. I'm not understanding a word you're telling me." Police Chief Alex Theopoulos wore a bemused grin beneath his recently acquired mustache.

"At the . . . at the inn," David sputtered.

"There was this open door and he was there," said Sebastian.

"There. On the bed."

"Who was on the bed?" Alex asked.

"This guy," said Sebastian. "He was—"

"It was gross." David's face made Alex laugh.

"Gross," Alex repeated. "You say Corrie was with you?"

The boys nodded.

"Where is she? Maybe I can get some sense out of her."

"She went home first," said Sebastian. "She's meeting us here. I can explain."

"But—"

"David, let me tell. You'll just get the hiccoughs again."

Alex glanced across the room to see if his deputy was listening. Rebecca Quinn raised her eyes to meet Alex's and stifled a laugh. Distracted, Alex asked, "Have you boys met my new deputy? Rebecca, say hello to Sebastian Barth and David Lepinsky, two fine young citizens and outstanding detectives to boot."

Rebecca Quinn smiled. Sebastian couldn't help noticing how beautiful she was. She seemed too refined, too delicate, to be even a television cop; in real life, the combination of her looks and her profession was almost shocking.

"Pleased to meet you," said Sebastian.

"Yeah," David said in an offhand way. "See, that's the point. About us being detectives."

"Right," Sebastian said. "We found a body. That's what we've been trying to tell you."

"You found a body." Alex drew the words out, using them to build a bridge from his personal to his official self. "You're not kidding around, are you?"

"Thanks a lot," said Sebastian. "In ten seconds, we've gone from being fine young citizens to liars."

"Sorry," Alex said, shaking his head. "Of course you're telling the truth. It's just, I get kids playing pranks sometimes, so I . . . but not you two, I should know better. Tell me again, from the beginning. Sit down, take a breath, and tell me what happened."

By the time Corrie arrived, Alex and his deputy had heard the story twice. After the first telling, Alex had reprimanded the boys for trespassing. Then he admitted that he'd always been the curious sort himself and would probably have been as incapable of staying away from that open window as they had been.

"Corrie," Alex said, after hello, "I've already asked Sebastian and David this. Now it's your turn. Are you sure the person you saw was dead? Let me

25

rephrase that. Are you sure there was a person on the bed?"

"Oh, yes," said Corrie without hesitating.

"Did you see his face?"

Corrie nodded.

"Describe it," Alex said.

"It was a face. I don't know. . . . It was dark in the room and—did they describe it?" She indicated Sebastian and David.

Alex smiled. "Uh-uh," he said. "No fair. You describe it; never mind what they said."

"I—I don't know if I can. Like I said, it was dark and the light was on for just a few seconds. But there *was* someone there. I know what you're thinking. It was something else on the bed and we imagined it was a person. But I saw the face, a man's face. . . ." Corrie spoke slowly now, taking time to re-create the scene in her mind's eye. "He didn't have a beard, but he was kind of stubbly, whiskers, you know. His hand was hanging over the side of the bed."

"What did his hand look like?" asked Alex. "Was it big? Did he have long, thin fingers or short, stubby ones? Was he wearing any jewelry?"

Corrie thought for a moment. "I don't know. I don't remember anything about his hand except the way it was hanging there." She shuddered to think of it.

"Was there a blanket over him?" Corrie looked up at the sound of Rebecca Quinn's voice, and Alex made a quick introduction.

"A blanket? I don't think so."

"What was he wearing?"

"I don't know. A jacket, maybe, or a shirt."

"It was a shirt," Sebastian said suddenly. "I re-

26

member. A red-and-black one, the kind you wear hunting."

"All right," Alex said. "Now I'll ask the other part of my question. How do you *know* he was dead?"

"Either he was dead or a *very* sound sleeper," said Sebastian. "After we saw him, we all started shouting and I dropped the flashlight on the floor. When I found it and turned the light on again, he hadn't moved."

"You're sure?"

Sebastian nodded vigorously.

"Without a doubt?"

"Without a doubt."

Alex and Rebecca exchanged a look. "All right," the police chief said, "let's go."

"With pleasure," said Rebecca. "It's so hot in here I can hardly breathe. Isn't there any way to regulate this heat?"

Alex just laughed.

"Are we going back to the inn?" David asked.

"We are," said Alex, emphasizing the pronoun and indicating his deputy with a nod.

"Shouldn't we come with you?" Sebastian asked.

Alex told him he didn't think that would be such a good idea. "You were lucky the first time," he said. "There could be someone else lurking around the place. And if this is a case of foul play, that someone might not be very nice."

"But don't you need us as witnesses? What if someone has been there since we left? We could tell you if anything has been moved or messed with."

"He may be right," said Rebecca Quinn. "Why don't they stay in the car while we go inside and

27

search? If we need them, it'll be a lot easier having them nearby."

Alex frowned. It was clear he didn't love the thought of having three kids along, but he also recognized Rebecca's point as valid. "All right," he said. "On two conditions. One, we call your parents and make sure it's all right with them. And two, you stay in the car with the doors locked."

"Agreed," said Sebastian.

"You got it," David said.

Corrie nodded, glad to be going along, but even gladder she was being spared another look at the corpse.

As it turned out, Corrie was not the only one to be spared.

Sebastian rolled down the patrol car window as soon as he saw Alex and Rebecca making their way back from searching the inn. It felt as if they'd been gone forever.

"There's no body," Alex announced.

"What?"

"We searched all the rooms," said Rebecca. "There's no one there. Dead or alive."

Sebastian and his friends exchanged bewildered looks.

"But we *saw* him," David said.

Alex got the same bemused expression on his face he had worn earlier. This time, it was mixed with a small measure of annoyance. "I'm afraid you *thought* you saw him," said Police Chief Alex Theopoulos. "It's easy to convince yourself you're seeing things when you're alone in a dark house."

"But we weren't alone," said Sebastian. "There were three of us, and we all saw the same thing."

"That happens, too," Alex said. His dismissive tone of voice as he opened the car door and slid into the driver's seat made Sebastian angry. He and his friends were not playing pranks. Nor were they imagining things. Whether or not he was there now, someone had been lying on that bed. Sebastian had to find a way to convince Alex that that much at least was true.

"Can we go back in the house with you?" he asked.

Alex's hand hesitated on the ignition key. "In the daylight," he said into the rearview mirror. "Meet us at the station at one o'clock tomorrow. Rebecca, do you mind putting in a couple of hours on your day off?"

"I don't if you don't."

"Settled," said Alex. He started the car and repeated, "Tomorrow. One o'clock."

9

It was two minutes to one. Josh Lepinsky, his hands warming in the pockets of his heavy corduroy pants, moved briskly across the village green. Sebastian, David, and Corrie had to run to keep up with his pace. They were all relieved to reach the door of the police station, but their relief vanished the moment they entered.

"Welcome to the Pembroke Sauna!" Alex pulled himself up from the desk, where he was going through some papers, and lumbered toward them. "Your tax dollars at work."

"They're working overtime," said Josh, peeling off his down vest. He nodded toward the kids. "The tribunal of parents conferred last night and decided one of us should be present this afternoon," he informed the chief, who, aside from Sebastian's mother and father, was his closest friend. "After hearing about your new deputy, I felt it should be me."

Alex laughed. Josh had been a widower for some time, but it was only in the last couple of years that he'd shown any interest in dating. "I'd call you a wolf," Alex said, "except wolves have more hair."

"Do you think she'll notice?" Josh asked, running a hand over his bald spot.

"Notice, yes," said Alex. "Care, no. Ah, here she

30

is now. Rebecca, come meet our local celebrity. This is Josh Lepinsky, author of the famous Flinch detective novels. Josh, Rebecca Quinn, former Miss Teenage New Hampshire, graduate of Boston College—Phi Beta something, third-generation cop, and newly appointed deputy chief of police, Pembroke, Connecticut."

"I'm impressed," Josh said.

The deputy's eyes brightened as she extended her hand to shake Josh's. "I'm a fan of yours," she said. "I loved *The Case of the Enigmatic Fortune Cookie.*"

"Now I'm even more impressed," said Josh.

"I had no idea you lived in Pembroke," Rebecca told Josh. "Alex, you've been keeping secrets."

"Yes, Alex," said Josh, not taking his eyes off Rebecca, "you've been keeping secrets."

"I'm charged with protecting the public interest," said Alex. "I thought I was doing my civic duty by not letting Rebecca meet you."

"I'm the public, too," Josh said. "What about my interests?"

David cleared his throat. "Excuse me," he said. "Before we all melt, weren't we supposed to look for a body this afternoon?"

"I think it's cute," Corrie whispered to Sebastian.

David shot Corrie a look that said, I may puke.

"Right," said Alex, "let's go. Rebecca, why don't you take Josh in your car? The kids can ride with me."

"Do you think your parents would mind if I moved in with you?" David asked Sebastian as they were leaving. "I don't know if I can stand being in the same house with a father who's going through writer's block and adolescence at the same time."

31

Sebastian laughed. "Who knows?" he said. "Maybe being in love will inspire him."

"Right," said David. *"The Case of the Brain That Turned to Mush."*

"This is it!" Josh cried as they entered the inn. "Inspiration at last! A body found in an abandoned inn. *The Case of ... The Case of ...*"

"Corrie had a good one," said Sebastian. *"Dew Drop Dead."*

Josh snapped his fingers. *"Dew Drop Dead!* I love it. Do you mind if I use it, Corrie?"

"I don't mind," Corrie said, looking with a mixture of fond and uneasy familiarity at the grandfather clock in the front hall, "but, well—"

"What?" Josh asked.

"It doesn't seem like something to kid about anymore," she said. "I mean, somebody really died here. We saw a body."

Josh's face immediately sobered. "You're right," he said. "I guess I'm still assuming it was all a misunderstanding. Are you sure what you saw wasn't just a bunched-up blanket or something?"

"Dad," said David, "We've been through this. How many times do we have to tell you guys? There *was* a body."

The chandelier suddenly blazed with light. A moment later, Alex entered from the area of the kitchen. "I just threw the switch," he said. "I had the electricity turned on this morning."

"On a Sunday?" asked Josh, surprised. "That's service. What I want to know is, if you coppers can get the lights turned on in an abandoned house on a Sunday morning, how come you can't get anybody to regulate your heat?"

Alex shrugged. "There are some mysteries in this world that are destined to remained unsolved," he said. "That's one of them."

"It's dark as night upstairs," Rebecca pointed out. "We had to have more light to investigate properly. We've already been out here once this morning."

Alex caught the look of surprise on Sebastian's face.

"I'm sorry, Sebastian," he said. "But I wasn't having you kids walk into a dangerous situation. We did find some evidence to support your notion that someone has been here, though. Want to take a look?"

"Sure," said Sebastian.

As the kids climbed the stairs, they couldn't help thinking how different everything appeared with the lights on. Sebastian wondered if his friends were thinking, as he was: Maybe we *did* imagine it.

But when they stood at the threshold of the bedroom, he knew they'd imagined nothing. It was true no one was lying on the bed this morning, but that was just the point.

"If it had looked like this yesterday," Sebastian said, "don't you think that's how we would have remembered it? I'm telling you, a man's body was right there."

"He was on his back," said Corrie. "With his arm hanging over the side."

"The flashlight fell here." David pointed to a spot by Sebastian's left foot.

"I believe you," said Alex.

"You do?"

33

"Yes. I have no doubt that someone was here. It's obvious even at a glance around the room. Look at the indentation on the pillow, the way the blankets are disturbed. Look at all the bottles under the bed. And there in the corner." He pointed to a heap of liquor bottles and crumpled-up bags spilling over with empty food containers and cigarette packs.

"Someone was living here," said the deputy. "Our guess is that a homeless man—or woman, although it appears to have been a man—discovered the inn and had the idea, a good one at that, to call it home."

"There are other signs of life," Alex said. "The bathroom down the hall has been used. And there are cigarette butts and remains of food downstairs as well."

"I'm amazed the place isn't crawling with rats," Josh said.

"It may be," said Alex. "We just haven't seen any."

Corrie felt a chill run down her spine. Rats.

"But the body—" Sebastian said.

"Our theory on that," said Alex, "is that you *did* see a body here last night. Not a *dead* body, but an unconscious one. It doesn't appear that whoever was living here had been around very long. At the same time, look at the number of bottles. He was obviously a heavy drinker."

Rebecca nodded. Clearly, she and Alex had talked the whole thing over earlier. "We think your 'corpse' was someone sleeping off a serious drunk," she said. "He was so out of it he never heard you, so he never moved."

"But if he didn't hear us," Sebastian said, "why wasn't he here when you came back later?"

"It's possible he was just conscious enough to have sensed someone was here and that he was in danger—the way we sense real sounds and events entering our dreams sometimes when we sleep. Or he may have simply awakened and left."

Alex reached into his pocket. "Here's something else to support your story. We didn't find it until this morning." He pulled out a small piece of red-and-black cloth. "This was caught on a nail sticking out of the sash of the dining room window. We assume the man left in a hurry, and this was torn on his way out. It matches what you described as the shirt worn by the person on the bed."

"From the look of it," Rebecca said, pointing out the small black button that was still attached, "we'd say it was ripped from the sleeve cuff."

"I can't believe it," David said. "Here we thought we saw a body and all it was was a stupid lush."

"Try not to sound so disappointed," his father told him.

"Really," Corrie said. "We should be glad whoever it was wasn't dead."

"Other than the fact that it's no longer occupied, is there anything different about this room from what you saw last night?" Alex asked, reaching to turn off the light.

Sebastian shook his head. "We didn't really look around much up here. We were mostly downstairs."

"Then let's take a look down there," said Alex.

As they were descending the stairs, Corrie asked, "What happens now?"

"We close the place up and try to find the owners," Alex told her.

"I don't mean that," Corrie said. "What happens

35

to the man who was staying here? This was his home."

"It wasn't really his home," Alex said. "No place is really his home, unfortunately. As for what happens to him now, that's a bigger question than I can answer."

Corrie looked back up the stairs and felt overwhelmed by sadness. She tried to imagine where the man was, but she couldn't even think what he looked like, who he might be. Her imagination failed her utterly.

"The magazine isn't here," she heard Sebastian saying. He was kneeling by one of the chairs in the sitting room. "There was a detective magazine lying here on the floor yesterday. I guess he took it with him."

"There's nothing like a good mystery," said Josh.

Sebastian stood. "Here's another one," he said.

"What's that?" Alex asked.

"A mystery. See all those photographs on the mantel? There was one of a family in front of a sailboat. It's gone."

"He must have taken that, too," said David. "That's weird. Why would he do that?"

Corrie studied the blank space on the mantel and said to herself, although loudly enough that the others heard, "Happy times."

10

On Monday morning, several members of the police department cleared the Dew Drop Inn of refuse and sealed it up with fresh sheets of plywood. A large sign was posted out front, along with smaller ones on the windows and doors: NO TRESPASSING BY ORDER OF THE PEMBROKE DEPARTMENT OF LAW ENFORCEMENT. VIOLATORS WILL BE PROSECUTED.

Corrie's father, fired up by her emotional recounting of what she'd seen at the inn and the police's theory of what had really gone on there, was even more determined to set up a program for the homeless at First Church. He asked Corrie if she would head a youth-group committee to work with the program, to which she readily agreed. The Reverend Wingate spent most of Monday on the phone to congregants, hoping, as he put it, "to light a fire under their sedentary behinds." After school, Corrie used the second phone line in the church office to call all the members of the youth group and tell them there would be a special meeting on Wednesday night. By five o'clock, she had fifteen people who said they would come—not counting herself, Sebastian, or David.

Monday was a busy day for Josh Lepinsky, too. Other than quick trips to the kitchen for coffee and his usual break around eleven to shoot the breeze with the mailman, he never left his office. His new Flinch mystery, *Dew Drop Dead,* was taking shape with an ease and energy he hadn't felt in months. He was as surprised as his children when he looked up at six o'clock and found them standing in his doorway.

"Aren't you going to stop?" Rachel asked plaintively. "What are you making for dinner?"

"A phone call," Josh answered. He jumped up, ordered pizza, and went back to work. While they were eating, he made another call, this one to Rebecca Quinn, allegedly to query a technical point about police procedure, the sort of thing he used to run by his friend Alex. Rachel and David exchanged knowing looks.

Later, David went across the street to Sebastian's house. "Nothing new," Sebastian told him, code for, "My dad hasn't lost his job yet and we're not moving anywhere." Upstairs in his bedroom, Sebastian told David about the program at First Church.

"Corrie called me an hour ago," he said, flopping down on one end of the bed and leaving room on the other end for David. "She wanted to know if we'd work with the youth group giving out food and clothes to homeless people."

"Why didn't she call me?" David asked.

"She wasn't sure you'd want to do it since you're not a member of the church." He didn't mention that Corrie had also told him she thought David had the social awareness of a slug.

"Are you going to do it?" said David.

"Sure."

"Then I will, too."

Sebastian smiled at the depth of his friend's motivation.

The boys fell silent for a minute, then David asked, "So what do you think, Sebastian? Do you believe it?"

Sebastian knew just what David meant. "No way," he said. "The guy was dead. You want to go out there with me tomorrow?"

"To do what?" David asked. "Alex said they were closing the place up tight as a drum."

"I don't know to do what," said Sebastian. "I just want to look around. Something isn't right. I have this hunch . . ."

He let the rest of the sentence drop. David knew from the faraway look in Sebastian's eyes that there was no point in asking what he'd been about to say. If David wanted to find out, he would just have to go with him. Back down Dead Man's Hill.

Back to the Dew Drop Inn.

WITHDRAWN
Speedway Public Library

11

"I can't believe you're going out there again," Corrie said with a curiously parental tilt of her head. The bell was about to ring for French class. "I'm not going with you."

"I didn't think you would."

"Really, Sebastian, that place gives me the creeps."

"You said you liked it."

"Not anymore. Besides, the case is closed." She opened her workbook to check a page of homework, then looked up to find Sebastian staring at her. "Isn't it?"

Sebastian heard the sound of their teacher's voice out in the hall. "You know as well as I do there was a dead body on that bed," he whispered, turning in his seat and leaning across Corrie's desk so no one else would hear.

"Ooo, look at the lovebirds," Adam Wells called out from across the room. Sebastian zapped him with a rubber band.

"I'm not so sure," Corrie said in a hushed voice. "I think Alex is right. The man was drunk. He never heard us, that's all. Besides, where did he disappear to? Corpses don't just get up and walk away."

Sebastian was about to attempt an answer when there was a loud and violent *B-R-R-R-R!*

"Mes amis, mes amis!" the French teacher sang out in a voice slightly discordant with the bell's reverberation. *"Comment allez-vous aujourd'hui?"*

"Très bien, merci," the class droned in unison, sounding anything but.

"I don't know," Sebastian said softly as he turned back in his seat. "Maybe *this* corpse did walk away."

"Qu'avez-vous?" the teacher asked of Sebastian. "What is the problem, Monsieur Barth?"

"Nothing," said Sebastian. "I mean, *rien.*"

"Bon," the teacher said, turning to pick up a piece of chalk and face the board. *"Allons-y.* Today, the relative pronoun."

"Rien," Sebastian muttered to himself. *"Rien* but a walking corpse."

12

By late Tuesday afternoon the temperature had dropped again, and although it was only a week into November, winter was in the air and fast working its way into the bones. The grounds of the Dew Drop Inn were covered with fallen leaves and frostbitten weeds that crackled as the two boys made their way, step by careful step, over them.

"I still don't know what we're supposed to be looking for," David called out, his voice muffled by the collar of the turtleneck sweater he'd pulled up over his mouth.

"I'm not sure either," Sebastian called back.

David stopped in his tracks. "Great!" he shouted. "I schlepp all this way, figuring you'll tell me what we're doing once we get here. And now you say you don't know! This is crazy! *You're* crazy!"

Sebastian didn't look up as he continued his search. "I didn't say I didn't know what we were doing, I said I wasn't sure what we were looking for. Listen, if there *was* a dead body on that bed Saturday afternoon and there *wasn't* a dead body on that bed Saturday night, and if there is no sign of that dead body anywhere in the inn, then . . ."

He stopped speaking and arched his back, twisting his neck from side to side. Even at a distance,

David could hear the bones in Sebastian's neck crack.

"Then?"

"Then the body must have been removed. Right?"

"If you say so."

"In which case, there should be some kind of evidence that the body was removed. Right?"

"If you say so. Just one thing."

"What's that?"

"How come we're looking for evidence and the police aren't?"

Sebastian waited for one last crack, straightened his neck, and began scanning the ground again. "Because," he said, "they subscribe to one theory— the theory of the drunk in the bed—and I subscribe to another."

"Which is the theory of what?"

"Murder."

"Oy vay," said David.

"What'll you give me if I'm right?" Sebastian asked.

"My sister," David said. He lowered his eyes to the ground and resumed looking for anything that might be considered evidence. Even though he found nothing very interesting, he glanced at the boarded-up windows from time to time and wondered if Sebastian was right. That body had looked awfully dead to him, too.

"What's this?" he heard Sebastian say. He went running. Sebastian was crouched over a crumpled red-and-white wrapper.

"An empty cigarette pack," said David. "Don't tell me you're going to say *that's* evidence. I've spotted

43

about ten of them already. Besides, dead men don't smoke."

"Murderers might. But you're right. There's nothing conclusive there."

"There's nothing conclusive anywhere," said David with a shiver. "I think it's gotten ten degrees colder in the last five minutes. Can we go home now?"

Sebastian stood and regarded the inn once more. "Let's start at the dining room window and walk over to the woods," he said, as if David hadn't spoken. "The window was the only way out before Alex came and opened the front door."

"Um, excuse me," David said. "I'm cold."

"We'll go in five minutes," Sebastian promised, and he crossed to the dining room window.

David watched Sebastian walk away and wondered, What if he was right? What if the murderer *had* left by that window? It was the same window, he told himself, that they'd used to get into the inn. What if the murderer had been in there with them the whole time?

What if the murderer was watching them now?

It was dark when they reached the edge of the woods and Sebastian finally conceded that their search had been a futile one. David, who by this time had convinced himself his friend might not be so crazy after all, had really tried to find something, anything, to prove it. But there was nothing to be found.

"Unless," Sebastian said, completing an unspoken thought, "we're missing something. Or unless . . ." He hesitated, hating to admit the possibility. "Unless," he repeated, "Alex is right and I'm wrong."

Ordinarily, David would have slapped Sebastian on the shoulder and said with a laugh, "Don't feel bad, Sherlock. The police have to be right sometimes." But now, as he stood looking into the woods, whose barren trees reached up to grasp at the moon with bony fingers, he couldn't quite let go of the possibility that Sebastian, despite his doubts and the lack of evidence, was on to something.

He shivered again. This time it had nothing to do with the cold.

13

"So where are the refreshments?" Adam Wells said indignantly. "I came for the refreshments."

It was seven twenty-five on Wednesday. The meeting of the First Church Youth Group had been called for seven, and so far only six people had shown up. Three of those six were Corrie, Sebastian, and David. Corrie was in no mood for the likes of Adam Wells.

"There *aren't* any refreshments," she snapped. "This is a meeting about hunger, Adam. I didn't think it was exactly appropriate to serve punch and cookies while we talked about starving children."

"Okay, okay." Adam shrugged and took a seat in the large circle of mostly empty folding chairs. His jaw dropped when he saw whose spindly legs were sprawled out across from his.

"Harley!" he said.

"So?" said Eddie "Harley" Davidson. Corrie herself had not quite gotten over the fact that one of the few people who'd managed to come to her meeting was none other than the former leader of the Devil Riders and one of the toughest kids in the eighth grade. Even now, while Harley clenched his fists as if ready for a fight, she wondered why he was here—and if he'd be trouble. She had never seen him anywhere near the church before; she'd called him only because his name was on her list.

"Nothing," Adam said. "I was just saying, 'Harley!'—you know, like 'Hey, Harley, how's it going?' "

"Yeah, right," said Harley, his fists still tight, hard balls.

"Um, how about starting the meeting, Corrie?" said Janis Tupper, the sixth person in attendance. "I've got to study, y'know?"

"Me, too," Corrie said with a sigh. "I was just hoping more people would show up. I don't get it. There were supposed to be eighteen people here."

"Lesson number one," said Harley. "Don't count on nobody for nothing."

"Well," Corrie said, "I hope I can count on all of you!"

"You can count on me if you serve refreshments," Adam said. "Anybody got any gum?"

Corrie cleared her throat and set about explaining why this meeting had been called. In the state of Connecticut, she told them, over ten thousand people had stayed overnight in shelters in just one recent six-month period. Those people accounted for only a fraction of the homeless. There were others who lived with relatives, in welfare hotels, in abandoned buildings, or on the street. Some were displaced mental health patients; others were out of work and destitute.

"These people need help," Corrie said. "That's why my dad set up this program—to give food, shelter, and clothing to anyone who's in need."

"How do you know who's in need?" Adam said, chomping on his wad of gum as if it were a juicy

47

steak. "I mean, anybody could walk in here and help themselves to clothes and food and stuff."

"That's the point," said Corrie. "Anybody can. The philosophy of the program is: If they come here, they're needy."

"But—"

"No forms to fill out, no questions asked." She looked down at her notes, intending to move on quickly before Adam could interrupt. "The youth group is going to help sort the clothes that will be coming in, make sandwiches on Saturday mornings, and give out the food at lunchtime."

"Hey, Sebastian," Harley said, "we should be good at that."

Sebastian gave Harley a thumbs-up. The two boys worked together as volunteers in the school cafeteria. Sebastian hadn't realized before how much pride Harley took in his position there.

Corrie cleared her throat and said, somewhat sheepishly, "I had planned on asking half the group to come Friday night to sort clothes and the other half to come Saturday morning, but with so few people—"

"Don't sweat it," Harley said with a wave of his hand. "We'll all be here."

Corrie looked at Harley in amazement. *"Both* times?" she said.

"I can't come Friday night," said David. "But I'll be here Saturday."

"What about everyone else?" Corrie asked. No one spoke. "Great. I'll see you at seven on Friday then. And listen, if you can get anyone else to come, we need all the help we can get."

As the meeting broke up, Corrie noticed Sebastian and Harley talking by the door.

"I still can't believe it," Corrie said when she and Sebastian and David were the only ones left. Her hand was on the light switch as she checked the room to be sure she wasn't leaving anything behind. "I never thought Harley would come. All he said on the phone was maybe. Why *did* he, do you think?"

She turned out the light, and Sebastian said, "He told me."

"What did he say?" Corrie asked.

"He said with all the do-gooders around, he figured what you really needed was an expert."

"An expert?" said David. "What's that supposed to mean?"

"It means he would never have asked the question Adam did. It means—how did he put it?—that he knows what it's like to hurt bad and have nowhere to turn."

14

The cat with no tail ran to meet Sebastian at the front door of his house.

"Hey, Chopped Liver," Sebastian said, bending down to scratch the cat behind his ears. "Where is everybody?"

"I'm here."

Sebastian looked up to find his grandmother standing in the doorway between the living room and the front hall, her reading glasses in one hand, an open book in the other. She regarded Chopped Liver and shook her head. "That cat thinks it's a dog," she said predictably.

"Maybe he's *part* dog," said Sebastian. "He was a stray, don't forget." Then, putting his hand to the side of his mouth so as not to offend Chopped Liver, he added in a stage whisper, "We don't know anything about his family background."

"Oh, Sebastian," Jessica Hallem said, pulling her lips back in a tight approximation of a smile, "You're such a tease."

"Well, it's good to see somebody smiling around here."

Immediately, the smile disappeared. His grandmother's face looked tired, worn-out in a way Sebastian was not used to seeing. She walked back into the living room where Sebastian found her, moments later, sitting in a solitary pool of light, reading or attempting to.

"Where are Mom and Dad?" he asked, balancing a glass of milk and a plate of cookies. All Adam's talk about refreshments at the meeting had left him famished.

"Out."

Sebastian put the cookies down on an end table.

"Coaster," his grandmother reminded him.

He reached into a drawer and removed a small straw mat to place under the glass of milk. "Where?" he asked.

"Your father had to attend to something at the station. Then your mother decided—all of a sudden—that her evening manager, who has, I believe, more years' experience in the business than your mother, could no longer handle the restaurant alone."

"What's going on, Gram?" Sebastian asked. "Mom and Dad hardly tell me anything anymore. And the way they're always getting at each other—it's not like them, you know?"

Jessica tucked a flap of her book between the pages where she'd been reading and thoughtfully took her glasses off and laid them in her lap.

"It isn't that the situation doesn't warrant a certain amount of drama," she said, "but I do feel your mother and father are laying it on a bit thick these days." Her cool tone was more that of a critic than a concerned member of the family. "I have told Katie that if Will must relocate for the sake of his work, she has no choice but to sell her restaurant and go with him."

"To which she said?"

51

"That I was living in the nineteenth century."

Sebastian smiled. "Oh, yes," his grandmother said. "Go ahead, be amused. She thought I was funny, too. 'Quaint' was the word she used. But I see nothing quaint about peace in the family. What disturbs me more than the situation itself is how your parents are—or perhaps I should say, are *not*— coping with it."

Hearing the word a second time, Sebastian asked, "What exactly is the situation, Gram? Do you think Dad's going to lose his job?"

Jessica sighed heavily and clucked her tongue. "I am an avid reader of the Bible and the *Wall Street Journal*," she replied obliquely. "I can't help thinking it would take a miracle such as the ones recorded in the former to help reverse some of the trends reflected in the latter. Sebastian, the hand of the mighty corporation is upon little WEB-FM and has the force, I fear, of a tidal wave. I do not imagine Will Barth will remain standing in its wake."

"In other words—"

"In other words, it seems almost certain that Herself is selling the station. And despite assurances from the prospective buyer, I have read too often that when this kind of takeover occurs, it is only a matter of months, sometimes weeks, until new management is in place. And old management, meaning your father, is not even given a gold watch for its trouble. A curt thank-you and 'here's your hat' are more like it."

It was Sebastian's turn to sigh. He had lived his whole life in Pembroke. He hated the idea of moving. Especially now, what with Corrie and all.

"I'm sorry, Sebastian," Jessica said. "It really

52

isn't fair for you to have to bear the burden of all this."

"Sure it is," Sebastian answered. "It's my family. And I already lost my radio show because of 'all this,' didn't I? Besides, I'm not five years old anymore."

His grandmother's smile was softer, a truer one this time. "No," she said, "you're not. Much as it amazes me at times, you are no longer a child."

Their second cat, a black one named Boo, entered the room and, seeing that Sebastian was home, promptly claimed his lap.

"And how was the meeting at the church?" Jessica asked.

Sebastian gave his grandmother a detailed description of the program the Reverend Wingate had set up, along with the youth group's part in it.

"I am glad for your sake," she said when he stopped to take a breath, "that you're involved in something you find worthwhile. Personally, I can't see that a handout does these people much good."

"But if they're hungry—"

"They should find work."

"And if there isn't work?"

Jessica Hallem waved her hand in the air. Sebastian sensed that their conversation was drawing to a close. "Fiddle-faddle," she said. "There is *always* work for those who want it."

"Even Dad?" Sebastian asked.

"Absolutely," said his grandmother in a no-nonsense tone. "My goodness, Sebastian, don't compare your father with . . ."

She did not complete her sentence, for which Sebastian was grateful. As she picked up her book and resumed reading, he bit into a chocolate pecan cookie his grandmother had baked earlier that day and wondered if she had been hungry even once in her life.

15

On Saturday morning, when the world was still dark, Corrie woke to the sounds of tires crunching gravel and a motor cutting off. She wrapped a blanket around her and crossed to the window overlooking the driveway to see who was there. By the outdoor lamp, which apparently had been left on all night, she made out her father emerging from the church van, stretching his large frame so that it seemed like a giant's, then dropping his arms and looking amazingly small. Corrie glanced at the clock glowing on her night table.

5:52.

Where in the world had he been?

"Good morning, Peaches," said Junior Wingate, surprised to find his younger daughter standing at the bottom of the stairs waiting for him. "What are you doing up so early?"

"What are *you?*"

"I haven't been to bed."

"What's wrong?" Corrie asked in alarm.

"Sshh. Let's not wake the house. Come to the kitchen. I'll explain while I make some coffee and try to get warm. Just walking from the car, I'm chilled to the bone."

As the coffee percolated—a sound Corrie loved because she associated it with those rare and quiet mornings when she sat with her father and they talked about things that mattered—Reverend Wingate spread his hands out on the Formica tabletop and told his daughter all that he had done and seen that night.

"I had no idea," he began, "how many people there are living in boxes and sheds and newspaper cocoons." His usually melodious tones were tempered by sleeplessness, his range flattened, his voice raw. But at the core of his words there burned a passion that flared up from time to time, much as the last ember flares in a dying fire, fighting extinction, sending some small heat into a cold and sleepy world.

"I couldn't wait for the needy to come to us," he said. "When I heard how bitter it was going to be last night, I gathered up all the sweaters and coats and winter gear you kids had sorted out and called a couple of the regulars to meet me at the church at eleven." "Regulars" was how Corrie's father referred to the handful of congregants who could be counted on to say yes, no matter what the question. "We made sandwiches and packed them along with the clothes. And then we headed out looking for people to give them to."

He stopped speaking for a moment and rubbed his hands. "We didn't see anyone at first. After close to an hour, I began to wonder if I'd exaggerated this thing way out of proportion. After all, this isn't New York City or even Troy. Did I really think there were people sleeping on park benches in pretty little Pembroke? I entertained the notion that I'd invented the plight of the needy as a way to be needed. And then

I noticed something we'd probably passed right by a half-dozen times before. A pair of feet in mismatched shoes were sticking out of the end of a packing carton. I understood then that we needed to be looking with different eyes.

"We covered as much ground as we could and found twenty-three people in all. One family, Corrie—five people—live in a car on a dirt road off Route Seven. There were children huddled and shivering under a greasy blanket in the backseat. I gave them sweaters and mittens and hats. And they just stared at me, as if they had no idea what I was doing there. Or what they were doing there."

Junior Wingate fell silent, his eyes no longer looking at his daughter. They seemed to be staring through the walls at the wind that rattled the windows, and they grew hard, as if it were not the wind they were seeing but an enemy, lurking.

Corrie got up and poured him a cup of coffee.

He took the cup and closed his hands around it. "I told every one of the people we found that there was a place for them at the church," he said.

"How long can they stay there?" Corrie asked.

"As long as they need to. It's a temporary solution at best, Corrie. What they need is a permanent shelter. And we'll work on that. But we can't wait for all the pieces to be in place. We have to do the best we can with what we have. Maybe I'm a fool, but right now I can't worry about next week or the week after that. Winter is no longer coming; it is here."

Corrie looked at her father as he blew steam from his cup of coffee. His round face with its red cheeks and glasses forever slipping down his nose gave him the appearance of an overgrown kid. She knew that

57

some people had trouble taking him seriously, that they called him an idealist and told him teasingly— even though they weren't teasing—that he should grow up.

Was he a fool? she wondered.

He noticed her watching him. "A penny for your thoughts," he said.

She waited until her thoughts found words before answering. "I was just thinking," she told him, "that it's lucky for the world there are fools in it."

16

Down the street, Josh Lepinsky was making breakfast and, for the first time in weeks, whistling.

Sebastian, who finished his paper route a little after seven each morning and frequently joined his across-the-street neighbors for breakfast, heard Josh's unique blend of bluejay and blues as he dropped his bike against the back gate and hurried to the kitchen door.

"You're in a good mood," Sebastian observed, closing the door behind him and stamping his feet to warm them. The numbness in his toes turned prickly.

"That I am," said Josh. He handed Sebastian a mug of steaming hot chocolate.

Sebastian nodded his thanks. "How come?"

"Sit, sit," Josh said. "I'm concocting something out of a cookbook. At the rate I'm going, you may be eating your breakfast for lunch."

"I'm too cold to sit. So?"

"So?"

"So how come you're in such a good mood?"

"Ah, well. On the one hand, no more writer's block. Flinch is on the case again!"

"And on the other hand?"

"Pimento, pimento," Josh mumbled, his index finger resting on the open page of the cookbook. "Where am I going to find pimento at seven in the morning? Quick, Sebastian, what can I substitute?"

"I'm not sure what pimento is."

"I could use a fresh red pepper, I suppose. The question is, do I have any fresh red peppers?" He crossed to the refrigerator and, while searching its nether regions, told Sebastian, "I sent Flinch on vacation. Got him out of New York City. He's staying in a little Connecticut town, not unlike Pembroke, in an inn named, not so coincidentally, the Dew Drop Inn."

"Can you do that?" Sebastian asked. "Use the same name?"

"There's no copyright protection for names. Besides, the Dew Drop Inn is so common a name it's almost a cliché. So. One evening, Flinch agrees to a game of paddle tennis—"

"Paddle tennis?"

"In life, it's Ping-Pong. In certain kinds of mysteries, it's paddle tennis. Anyway, he agrees to a game the following morning with a gentleman staying in the next room. But when the gentleman is late for breakfast, lo and behold, it is discovered—"

"That the gentleman has been murdered."

"Dead in his bed. Soon all the guests are dropping like flies, and Flinch must solve the murders before he becomes the next victim. Ah-ha, pimentos!" Josh stood, a look of triumph in his eyes and a bottle of pimentos in his hand. "It's a change of pace, don't you think? I was getting a little tired of Flinch the hard-nosed cop shooting it out with drug dealers and hurling himself out of moving subway cars. Besides, this one is *funny*."

"I thought all your books were funny, Josh," said Sebastian.

Josh scowled for a fleeting second or two. "Well," he said, "yes. But this one is meant to be. Whoa! These pimentos smell like somebody's been wearing them for socks. Will you look at this? 'Use by August 31, 1982.'"

"The Case of the Putrid Pimentos," said Sebastian, feeling his nasal passages tighten. "So what's the other reason you're in such a good mood? On the one hand, no more writer's block. On the other hand—"

Two voices sang out as one: "Rebecca Quinn!"

Sebastian turned to see David and Rachel standing in the doorway.

"Ah, the angel choir," said Josh. "Guess what we're having for breakfast this morning, children."

David sniffed the air. "Cholera?" he ventured.

"Pancakes," Josh said over the roar of the garbage disposal. "Grab your coats. By the time we get back, the air should be fit to breathe again. You coming, Sebastian?"

"Sure," said Sebastian. "We're supposed to be at the church by nine-thirty, though."

"I don't see a problem there," Josh said. "Just don't anybody get fancy with their orders. No pancakes with pimentos."

"Or anchovies," Rachel said, taking her jacket from the coat tree in the hall.

"Or anchovies," Josh echoed as the disposal's roar quieted to a satisfied rumble. Just before switching it off, he swore he heard it burp.

17

The man in the far corner of the room called himself
Abraham. That was all he said or cared to say. "I
am Abraham."

He wouldn't take food or rest himself on any of
the cots that in the course of a few hours had trans-
formed the normally still and empty basement social
hall of First Church into a bustling dormitory for
the dispossessed. For over an hour, he had stood
there, rigid as a statue, clutching the bag he'd
brought with him.

As Corrie ladled out the soup Sebastian's mother
had donated, she chatted congenially with the people in line. Sebastian saw a side of her he'd never
seen before, how at ease she was in circumstances
that made him tense and uncertain. He glanced
across the room to where the Reverend Wingate was
inviting the homeless in as if they were old friends
come to visit, and the thought occurred to him that
Corrie was indeed her father's daughter.

A woman named Estelle Barker brought Sebastian's attention back to the task at hand. "You got
nothin' but tuna?" she asked in a loud and demand-
ing voice.

"Sorry?"

"Tuna. You got nothin' but tuna?" Estelle Barker

62

barked. And when he didn't answer, she said, "My boy here can't eat tuna. Makes him sick to the stomach. You got baloney?"

"Uh, no, I don't think so," Sebastian said. "Wait a minute."

"It's always the same," said Estelle Barker, gingerly lifting a slice of bread to inspect what lay beneath. "Everything is wait a minute, wait a minute, wait. Well, I got nothin' better to do. My life is on hold, anyway. What do I care?"

Sebastian entered the kitchen where his mother was supervising David and Harley in sandwich making. "I overheard," David said to his friend. "Gee, I guess beggars *can* be choosers."

"Now, David," said Katie, "the woman's got a right to food that doesn't make her son sick."

"But Mom," Sebastian said, "baloney?"

Katie shrugged. "To each her own. Why don't you take this plate of peanut butter and jelly? And there are some apples in that bowl we forgot to put out earlier."

"I'm surprised how many people showed up," Sebastian said, balancing the plate with one hand while he reached for the bowl with the other.

"Me, too," said David. "I hope we have enough sandwiches."

Harley laughed. "You guys crack me up," he said. "This isn't a party, y'know. We could stay here the rest of our lives making sandwiches, and there'd never be enough. You guys don't know nothing."

From the other room, Estelle Barker shouted, "That boy on a coffee break er what?"

Sebastian wondered for a fleeting moment if his grandmother had been right about "these people,"

63

but as he pushed open the door and caught sight of Estelle Barker's two young children pressed against her torn coat, he knew it was not his grandmother but Harley who had his finger on the truth.

"There you are! Now don't tell me you didn't find no baloney!"

Sebastian approached, his arms full of food but his words empty of salvation. "All we have is peanut butter and jelly," he said. "And some apples. There's soup—"

"Soup! Peanut butter!" Estelle Barker shook her head angrily. "My boy here, he got a sensitive stomach. He need his baloney."

Sebastian was wishing Corrie were there to help him out of what was threatening to turn into an embarrassing scene when suddenly an even greater commotion broke out elsewhere. He turned to see Corrie standing frozen in the center of the room. All eyes were on her, but it was the eyes of the man called Abraham that held her riveted to the spot.

The man's arms were twisted around the grease-stained shopping bag he clutched to his chest. His face was twisted, too, and out of his mouth came a torrent of twisted words—words that made no sense, a rush of babble spewed like lava, hot and suffocating.

"Don't you want something to eat?" Corrie asked. Sebastian saw now that she held a plate of food in her hands.

The man's cries were like something you might hear in the zoo, a caged animal suddenly remembering what it was to be wild. The look in his eyes as he stared unblinkingly at Corrie was so intense and so personal it made Sebastian want to look away, but he couldn't. He was spellbound.

Corrie held her ground. "No one's going to hurt you," she said in a gentle, unwavering voice. "I just thought you'd like to eat something. You look hungry."

The man's ranting came to an abrupt halt. He stood stock-still, his eyes narrowing to slits as he studied Corrie. After a moment, he loosened his hold on the bag. "I am Abraham," he growled.

It seemed to Sebastian as if the man were serving notice of some kind. But Corrie took it differently— or chose to, in any case. "I am Corrie," she said. "And I have food for you. Would you like it?"

"No."

"No, you don't want any food?"

"No, you are not Corrie."

No one spoke then, no one moved. The room itself seemed to hold its breath. Out of the corner of his eye, Sebastian noticed Corrie's father. The minister watched his daughter intently, yet he kept his distance. Suddenly, Estelle Barker's sharp voice cut through the tension like a knife.

"I'll take them peanut butter sandwiches," she said. "Maybe you have baloney another day."

Someone laughed at this, and Sebastian woke as if out of a dream. He gave Estelle Barker all the sandwiches she wanted. When he turned back a few minutes later, he saw that Corrie and the man called Abraham were seated on facing cots. It was the man who held the plate of food now, and he was eating.

18

Seven people slept in the basement of First Church that night: Estelle Barker and her two children, a soft-spoken man named Raymond Elveri, a woman with badly swollen feet who would not give her name, a teenager named Marcus who said he was on the run from a messed-up life, and the man called Abraham.

Having spent the entire day and the early evening at the church, Corrie arrived at Sebastian's house after dinner with a glow that was part elation, part exhaustion. It was the look of an athlete who has played hard and with determination; and in that context, it was a look Sebastian was used to seeing on Corrie's face. He knew that she had given her all to this day, as much or more than she had given to any game of football she'd ever played or any race she'd ever run.

He brought her into the sun room, where David was sprawled on a large floor pillow, studying the Scrabble tiles he'd just drawn.

"Is 'gluck' a word?" he asked without looking up.

"I doubt it," said Sebastian.

"No, I think it is," David said.

"Clue number one when you're playing with David," said Sebastian. "He gets that look on his face when he's lying."

"No, really. Gluck is the sound the lock on a suitcase makes." David mimed pressing a lock down with his thumb. "Gluck."

Sebastian raised his eyebrows. "Wrong, Lepinsky, gluck is the sound made by a hen with a speech defect."

"Gluck," said Corrie, getting into the swing of things, "is how an Australian says, 'Good luck'—'G'luck, mate.'"

Sebastian laughed and patted Corrie on the shoulder. "Excellent," he said. "Want some popcorn?"

Corrie shook her head.

"Glucose!" David cried, placing his tiles triumphantly on the board. He quickly added up his score and said, "You're dying here, Barth." Sebastian and David never called each other by their last names except when playing Scrabble.

Sebastian studied the score pad: 127 to 49. "You have an unfair advantage over me," he told his friend.

"I'd call being smart and well read an advantage but not unfair," David said.

"What I had in mind was that you play with Josh and he's a whiz at words."

"This is true," said David. Then, looking over the top of the wicker coffee table, he said, "Earth to Corrie."

Corrie had lowered herself to the floor and was leaning against the love seat, one hand absently petting the cat—she hadn't bothered to notice which one—who was rubbing against her legs. "Oh, sorry," she said. "I was just thinking about Abraham."

"What about him?" Sebastian asked, looking at his letters and wondering if there were any words in the English language that had no vowels.

"Oh, I was trying to figure him out, I guess. He wouldn't talk to anyone but me—I don't know why—and we talked for a long time, but I had trouble understanding what he was saying. My father says he's sick."

David grunted. "He's a psycho. Even I had that much figured out."

Ordinarily, Corrie would have given David a hard time for being so callous, but she couldn't argue with what he was saying. "I know. He is . . . different." David grunted again. "But I like him. He . . . Did I tell you what he calls me?"

"Let me guess," David said. "Saint Corrie of the Hot Lunch?"

"What?" Sebastian asked, begrudgingly putting C-A-T on the board and bringing his score up to an impressive fifty-two.

"Catherine the First. Isn't that weird? I don't know why. I kept telling him my name was Corrie, but he said, 'No, you are Catherine the First.' "

"Was she a queen or something?" Sebastian asked.

"I think there was a Catherine the Great," said David. "I don't know if there was a Catherine the First."

"I asked him if he had any family. He wouldn't answer. Then he said something about someone named Isaac. I said, 'Who's Isaac?' And he said, 'I am Isaac.' So I said, 'I thought your name was Abraham.' And he said, 'I am Isaac, I am Abraham.' See what I mean? Confusing."

"Sure," said David. "Stick with him and your brain will turn to cream cheese. Speaking of which, where are the refreshments—as Adam Wells would say?"

Sebastian shoved the bowl of popcorn across the rug. Boo lifted his head, jumped off Corrie's lap, and made a beeline for it.

"Yuck," David said. "Cat hairs in the popcorn. What else do you have?"

Later, during another round of Scrabble that included Corrie and two pints of ice cream, Sebastian asked if anyone wanted to go to the movies the next day.

"Sure," Corrie said.

"Maybe," said David. "I have something to do first."

"What?" Sebastian asked.

"Oh, just something."

Sebastian gave David a puzzled look. "What are you up to?" he asked.

David smiled and said, "You'll see." Then he laid his tiles out on the board. The letters read M-Y-S-T-E-R-Y.

"Triple word," said David. "That's forty-five points for the twelve-year-old. All *right!*"

19

The next afternoon, Sebastian and Corrie emerged from the pitch-blackness of the Pembroke Cineplex into the blinding light of day, their senses benumbed by relentless Dolby stereo and ninety-seven minutes in the company of screeching aliens with bad teeth. Corrie shrieked as a figure lunged out of the sunlight at them, then laughed when she saw it was only David.

"Get your bikes," David commanded. "I found something."

Sebastian, his mind still in a far-off galaxy, regarded his friend blankly as if he'd wandered in from another movie.

"I found something," David repeated.

"Where?" Corrie asked.

"The inn."

"What?" said Sebastian.

"Blood. Get your bikes."

20

"Blood? That's no blood!"

Sebastian and David were kneeling by a large rock about ten yards from the dining room window of the Dew Drop Inn. Corrie, hearing that the case of the disappearing body had been reopened, had elected to stay home. Sebastian was wondering if he shouldn't have done the same.

"What do you call it if it's not blood?" David asked indignantly.

Sebastian studied the spot on the rock's surface. "I call it a brown stain," he said. "It could be anything. It could be geological, for Pete's sake."

"What about this?" David said, pointing to a nearby clump of field grass caked with the same, or similar, brown substance.

"Like I said, it could be anything. I mean, *anything*, David. I wouldn't touch it if I were you."

David looked at his friend's face, then back at the inn. He felt his cheeks burn. "How come," he said after a moment's heavy silence, "when you get a hunch and follow it, it always leads to some brilliant discovery? But when I do the same thing, I end up feeling stupid."

"I didn't say you were stupid."

"You didn't have to. You're probably right anyway. It isn't blood. It's dog doodoo. And so's my case." He stood and walked a couple of feet away, staring at the dining room window.

"Listen," Sebastian said, "I believe as much as you do that there was a body on that bed."

David turned around. "Then why aren't you doing something about it?"

"Because, for once, I don't know what to do. We looked out here the other day and didn't find anything."

"We could break into the inn again."

"Wrong."

"I know."

"Besides," said Sebastian, "even though I told you the police weren't looking to find evidence of a murder, they *did* search the inn. You know Alex. If there was something to be found, he would have found it." Anticipating what David was about to say, he quickly added, "Maybe they didn't search out here, but we did."

"Yeah, and maybe we didn't search hard enough. That's why I came back. You got me thinking the other day, Sebastian. I think you're right. I *know* you are."

A gust of wind got the evergreens to whispering and Sebastian listened and wondered, *was* there a murder? If there was, maybe the answer was there—in the woods.

"Let's come back tomorrow," he heard himself saying. "After school. Okay?"

"Okay!"

Sebastian and David picked up their bicycles from where they'd let them fall ten minutes earlier. It was getting dark now—and colder. The wind had picked up. And the air was full of whispers.

21

Raymond Elveri brushed his gray-streaked hair each morning and made sure his fingernails were always clean and trimmed. "I still have my pride," Corrie had heard him telling the scruffy, sad-eyed Marcus the previous evening.

"Pride in *what?*" Marcus had snorted.

"Pride in my humanity" had been Raymond Elveri's answer.

Corrie had noticed that Raymond read the Bible a lot. He was not pompous about it, rarely quoted it, but it was clearly a source of solace to him. He looked up from time to time as he read, and Corrie could almost see his face grow younger and less troubled each time he did. She wondered about Raymond Elveri; she couldn't figure out what he was doing here. His clothes were worn but not tattered, his face clean-shaven, his rough hands those of a man who has known honest work.

When he saw Corrie come through the door of the social hall on Monday afternoon, Raymond smiled. He was sweeping the floor—"earning my keep," he told her—and the first thing he asked her was what it was like out.

"Cold," she said. "Don't tell me you've been inside all day."

"I know what you're thinking," he said. "It's not right for a grown man to be holed up like an animal in its den, hibernating, hiding from the world. I should go out; but I guess I just figure when I get out there, all I'll want to do is go back in. So I stay indoors and save myself the trouble. I polished the collection plates and altar rails this morning. I asked the Reverend, and he said that would be fine." Corrie wondered what John, the custodian, thought of it.

"You don't have to do all this work," she said.

"A man has to earn his keep," Raymond repeated. "Work is the natural order of things. Keeping busy is just keeping busy, but work is keeping busy with a purpose. Don't you agree?"

"I've never really thought about it," Corrie answered, sorry to disappoint him. She wanted to ask, "Why aren't you working then? Why don't you get a job?" But she couldn't bring herself to do that. She remembered his words: "I still have my pride."

Raymond, sensing her discomfort, resumed sweeping. Corrie took the opportunity to look around. In one corner of the room, Marcus sat straddling a chair turned backward, his head resting on his crossed arms, his eyes liquid and dreamy. She noticed that he was barefoot. It was after three. Had he even bothered to put on shoes today? In the other corner, Abraham lay on his cot, facing the wall. Even though the room was quite warm, he was wrapped in several blankets. She wondered if he were ill, then recalled that she had seen him like this once before. He must be cold-blooded, she thought. Or warm-blooded. She could never remember which was which.

Estelle Barker's bed was unmade but empty. She had taken her children, Corrie learned later, to "walk the mall," an activity that apparently occupied most of her days. The woman with the bad feet had left on Sunday morning and not returned.

"Where are your friends?" Raymond Elveri asked. He was dumping the contents of a dustpan into the large plastic garbage pail by the kitchen door.

"Janis has student council," Corrie said. She knew the friends Raymond meant, but since she didn't like what they were doing, she didn't want to have to talk about where they were.

"No, no, I mean the others," said Raymond. "That tall one is your boyfriend, I'll bet."

Embarrassed, Corrie shrugged. "I don't know," she said. "I guess. Kind of."

Raymond chuckled. "You're young," he said. "How old are you? Let me guess. Fifteen?"

"Not quite," Corrie said, pleased that he imagined her so much older than she was. "I'm thirteen."

Raymond seemed as pleased as she. "Thirteen!" he exclaimed. "My daughter—" He stopped speaking and turned away.

"Oh, you have a daughter?"

Raymond walked slowly to the supply closet and put away the broom. With his back to Corrie, he said in a voice so soft she wasn't sure she heard, "Two daughters. And a son."

Raymond Elveri had a family. What was he doing here?

"Where are they?" she asked.

Raymond's cot was the one next to Abraham's. He went to it now, sat on its edge, and pulled a Bible out from under his pillow. He didn't open it, just held it in his lap.

"They don't live in this state," he answered at last. The way he was bent over, he looked almost broken. What had become of his pride?

"Do they know you're here?" Corrie asked.

"Let's say they know I'm not there." Raymond looked up at her and for the first time his eyes looked as sad as Marcus's. "Corrie," he said, "you're thirteen, a long way from understanding the world and what it does to people. I wish you might never know, but that would be a waste of a wish. So what can I wish for you instead?" He thought for a moment, then said, "You look athletic. Are you a runner?"

"Yes."

"Then let me wish for you that you always run *toward* something, never away."

Corrie wanted Raymond Elveri to tell her what he was running away from. But she didn't want to ask. And she knew it wasn't any of her business, really.

She was trying to think of something else to say, something that would bring his smile back, make him forget whatever it was he had succeeded in forgetting but for her reminding him. She took her mind back to school, thinking there might be something in her day to interest him.

Before she'd found anything, the man called Abraham rolled over on his cot and cast a disdainful eye on Raymond's hunched back.

"The sins of the father," he said.

Raymond lifted the Bible to his heart and gripped it tightly.

22

"You realize we're looking for a needle in a hay-stack," Sebastian said as the boys moved their search deeper into the woods.

"Yeah," said David, "a needle dipped in blood."

"Give me a break," Sebastian said. "You're beginning to sound as melodramatic as—"

"As you used to?"

Sebastian frowned. "I was going to say your sister."

"Do you want to give up?"

"No way. Do you?"

David shook his head.

The wind didn't stir. The evergreens had ceased their whispering. No secrets, it seemed, would be revealed on this still and stillborn day.

Then Sebastian heard something. "Listen," he said.

David felt his pulse quicken, but he heard nothing. What was he listening for? Voices? Footsteps? What did danger sound like?

He tried again, but still he heard nothing.

Seeing his puzzled look, Sebastian said, "Water. There's a creek nearby."

"What are we, Indian scouts?" David asked. "I can't believe you got me all psyched just to tell me about a stupid babbling brook. I mean, it's poetic but—"

"The point is," said Sebastian, interrupting, "that the bed of a creek *might* have footprints. We sure aren't going to find any here."

David smiled meekly. "Right," he said. "I was just going to say the same thing."

The boys followed the creek for fifteen minutes, searching for footprints and finding none. When they came to a pool of water and what looked like the end of the creek, David said, "Do you have any idea where we are?"

"Nope," said Sebastian. "And it's getting dark. Maybe we should head back."

"Okay. But can we rest for a minute? These new sneakers are killing me."

"Strangled ankles?"

David grunted. "Feels like it. I brought an apple. You want half?"

"Sure," Sebastian said, resting on a rotted log that gave way under him. David laughed, then settled himself on a rock nearby, and the two boys fell silent.

Each held half an apple in his open hand, neither eating nor biting into it—not wanting, perhaps, to disturb this perfectly soundless universe in which they'd suddenly found themselves. The air was so still, the woods so devoid of any noise save their own breathing, that Sebastian said, although he thought he was only thinking it, "Fall's a kind of lonely time, isn't it?"

Then he glanced up and saw something. "There!" he shouted. "Look over there!"

A footprint, or three-quarters of one, wasn't ten

feet away. They ran to it, careful not to get so close they'd smudge it, and bent down to take a look. But before either of them could say, "It might mean nothing; it's only a footprint," David reached out his hand and picked up a small object lying nearby. It was a book, whose worn, brown leather cover had perfectly camouflaged it from their sight.

Both boys were smiling. "I think we hit the jackpot," Sebastian said. "Hurry up and open it."

"Easier said than done," said David. "It's all wet—the pages are stuck. Wait, I think I've got it."

But before he could say another word, Sebastian's fingers grabbed his arm. "Ow!" David yelled. "What's the matter with you?"

"We were right!" said Sebastian. His face grew pale, the color of the wind if the wind had a color. "We were right," he repeated. "We were right."

David didn't have to ask what he meant. He was almost afraid to look. When he finally dared, he no longer wanted to see. For there in a thicket of dark green trees, just a few feet behind the log where Sebastian had been sitting moments earlier, lay a body half-covered with leaves.

23

"I can't believe you found it," Corrie said not much more than an hour later. Sebastian and David had practically dragged her from her dinner table to tell her the news. Now she was squeezed between the two of them on the front steps of her house. "It gives me chills just imagining it."

"It gives *you* chills?" David said. "I don't even want to think about trying to sleep tonight. Nightmare city."

"Tell me everything," said Corrie eagerly.

David clutched his throat as if strangling himself. "The face was all blue and the tongue was sticking out like this and—"

"Well, maybe not *everything*. What happened after you found it?"

"We went right to the police station," Sebastian told her. "I don't think Alex believed us at first. But it didn't take long to convince him."

"Did he let you go with him to look for it?"

"Sure," said David. "What do you think? *We* were the ones who found it. We knew where it was."

It occurred to Sebastian that they were all referring to the body as "it." He guessed it was easier that way.

"It was dark by the time we got back there," he said.

"Who went?"

"Alex, Rebecca, and a couple other cops, I forget their names. They used these big, heavy-duty flashlights, and when they found it, they threw a light on its face and Alex asked, 'Is this the same person you saw lying on the bed at the inn?' "

"Oh, gross," said Corrie. "They made you *look* at it?"

"Just for a minute."

David said, "We told him, 'Yeah, that's the guy,' you know, like they do in the movies."

"But then we weren't sure. He wasn't wearing that red-and-black shirt."

"He wasn't?"

Sebastian shook his head. "And we never really got such a good look at the guy's face—I mean the one at the inn. So we told Alex we *thought* it was the same person."

"Then what happened? Did you watch them, you know . . ."

"Take away the body?" Sebastian asked. Corrie nodded. "Uh-uh. Alex said we should go back with Rebecca and she'd drive us home."

"What did your parents say?" Corrie asked, trying to imagine how her parents would have reacted. Not happily, she thought.

"Oh, they were okay," Sebastian said with a shrug of the shoulders. "They kept wanting to know if I was all right. I think they were worried I'd suffered some sort of trauma or something."

"Not my dad," said David. "He kept milking me

81

for details. That's the thing with writers: Everything is research."

"Now aren't you sorry you didn't go with us this afternoon?" Sebastian asked.

For the first time, Corrie smiled. "Are you kidding? I wouldn't have wanted to be there for *anything*. Besides, I had a good—well, interesting—time at the church. You want to walk over with me? I promised Mr. Elveri I'd come back tonight and show him some pictures."

"Pictures, what do you mean?"

"We got to talking about our families. And I was telling him about the vacation we took last summer, and he said he'd like to see pictures of it. You want to go with me?"

David looked doubtful, but Sebastian said, "Sure, why not? Looking at snapshots of Disney World will be a relief after the afternoon *we* had."

"Wait here. I'll get them and be right back."

When he saw Corrie enter with her friends, Raymond Elveri raised his eyes from his Bible and smiled warmly. "You remembered," he said.

"Of course I did," said Corrie. Looking to the next bed, she asked, "How are you tonight, Abraham?"

"I am within my body and my body is protected from the storm in this safe harbor."

"Good," said Corrie, seeming to know what he meant. David bit the inside of his cheek to keep from giggling. "Would you like to look at the pictures with us? I mean, is that okay with you, Mr. Elveri?"

"By all means. Abraham and I had a talk earlier this evening. He's not a bad person, you know, just a little confused at times. And frightened, like the rest of us."

"I know he's not bad," said Corrie.

Sebastian thought it was odd that they were talking about Abraham as if he weren't there. But he could tell from the serene look on Abraham's face that he wasn't offended. In fact, he looked more at peace than Sebastian had ever seen him.

They settled themselves on Raymond Elveri's cot, Raymond on one side of Corrie, Sebastian on the other. David sat next to Sebastian, and Abraham stood behind them, looking over Corrie's shoulder. "Would anyone else like to look at the pictures with us?" Corrie asked the others in the room.

The volunteer who was spending the night murmured, "No thanks," from where he sat across the room, then went back to his book.

Estelle Barker was watching the television that had been donated by one of the congregants. Glancing peevishly over her shoulder, she said, "I'm trying to watch my program. Don't talk too loud, hear?" Her two children lay on the carpet at her feet, their hands playing idly with the untied laces of her shoes. Every once in a while she swatted at them as if they were pesky flies, but she never told them to stop.

Marcus was stretched out on his cot nearby, his head resting on one hand, reading a magazine in the light that spilled off the television set. He didn't bother to look up at the sound of Corrie's voice.

"Okay," Corrie said, pulling the stack of photographs from their envelope. "Now, this first one was taken back in Troy before we left. See, my family just moved here this past summer. We lived in Troy, New York, before that and . . ."

Sebastian tuned out, not because he'd heard it all before, but because his attention was caught by a sight so disturbing his mind was busy struggling just to take it in. He nudged David and nodded in the direction of a chair sitting in the center of the room.

David exhaled, "Oh, wow."

A red-and-black shirt was draped over the back of the chair. Even from a distance, Sebastian could see that there was no button on the cuff of the left sleeve. In its place was a visible tear. There was no doubt about it: It was *that* shirt. Sebastian glanced around the room. Was the person they had seen at the inn—the one they *thought* was dead—here with them now?

Or, what was even more likely, was one of the people sharing this oddly warm and domestic scene in the basement of a church on a cold November night a murderer?

Sebastian looked from Estelle Barker's strong back to Marcus's furrowed brow to Raymond Elveri's rough hands to Abraham's knobby outstretched fingers and he wondered—

Who?

24

"Professor Plum in the billiard room with the lead pipe," said Rebecca Quinn. They were so engrossed in their game that neither she nor Josh nor Rachel looked up when Sebastian and David barged noisily into the Lepinsky kitchen.

"You guys," David said.

"Shut the door, it's freezing," said Josh. He waved a vague sort of hello and muttered, "Professor Plum, it can't be Professor Plum. And you call yourself a detective?"

"You guys," David repeated.

"Sshh," said Rachel.

Rebecca looked at Josh. "Sorry to disappoint you," she said. "I guess one murder case a day is all I can handle."

"Murder?" said Sebastian. "So you think it's murder, too."

Rebecca stretched. "Well, we don't have anything conclusive. We don't even know who the victim was. But murder looks like a definite possibility."

"How was the guy killed?" David asked.

"We think a blow to the head."

"Lead pipe?" asked Josh.

Rebecca smiled weakly. "No, and not in the billiard room either. We don't have the murder weapon yet."

"We do," David said. "It was a rock."

"A rock?" said Rebecca Quinn.

"You know what I mean, right, Sebastian? We found a rock with blood on it near the inn."

Josh looked from his son to his son's friend. "You saw it, too?" he asked.

Sebastian nodded slowly. "I'm not convinced it was blood," he told Josh and Rebecca. "It could be, but—"

"Gee, Sebastian, thanks a lot," said David. "What else could it be? We find this dead guy, and the police say he's been conked on the head, and there's a rock between him and the inn that's covered with this dark brown stuff and—"

"And then there's the shirt," said Sebastian. "That's what we came to tell you about."

Josh and Rebecca exchanged glances."Don't tell me you've found the murderer," Rebecca said.

"Yes!" David cried triumphantly.

Sebastian laid a hand on his friend's arm. "Slow down," he said. "We didn't find the murderer. But we think we know where you can find him. Or her."

Rebecca regarded Sebastian with interest. "Go on," she said.

"Well," Sebastian began, "remember that shirt we told you about? The red-and-black one?"

"The one we found a piece of at the inn," Rebecca said. "What about it?"

"We found the rest of it," said David excitedly. "We know it belongs to one of the people staying at the church. We just don't know who."

Rebecca raised her eyebrows. "Are you sure it's the same shirt?"

"Definitely," said Sebastian. "The sleeve is torn."

"There's a button missing," David added.

"And where exactly did you see it?"

"Hanging over the back of a chair. That's why we don't know who it belongs to," Sebastian answered. "But it has to belong to one of them, right?"

Rebecca thought for a moment. "Maybe not," she said.

"Huh?" said David.

"If we assume the murder victim was wearing the shirt and that the murderer removed it from his body after he or she killed him, we might also assume that the murderer threw it away."

"I don't get it," David said.

"The person at the church—whoever has the shirt now—might have found it somewhere. In a Dumpster, lying by the side of the road, wherever the murderer ditched it. I'm not saying you're wrong. But the shirt itself isn't conclusive evidence."

"Mrs. Peacock in the library with the candlestick," said Rachel.

"What?" asked Josh.

Rebecca turned to look at Rachel. "Sorry?"

"Mrs. Peacock in the library with the candlestick," Rachel said impatiently. "Are we playing or gabbing? Come on, you two, we've got a murder to solve here!"

"But you'll check out the shirt, won't you?" Sebastian asked Rebecca as the game was resumed.

"And the rock?" said David.

"You bet," Rebecca said. "We'll get on both of

them in the morning. First thing, we'll go out and take a look at that rock. As for the shirt . . ."

"Yeah?" David asked.

"Well, you might just be right. It could lead us to the murderer."

" 'The murderer,' " David repeated later in his room. The boys were sitting on either end of his bed. "Right now, right down the street in the basement of First Church, there could be a cold-blooded killer eating a peanut butter sandwich. We could have shaken hands with him or given him some soup or something. It's kind of cool, isn't it?"

"That's one way of looking at it."

"And just think, *we* found the body."

"Twice."

"Yeah, twice. I mean, the police wouldn't even have known there'd been a murder if it weren't for us. We found the body and the murder weapon, maybe, and *maybe* the murderer."

Sebastian pulled his knees up to his chin and fell silent.

"Oh, oh," David said. "Don't tell me you're going into one of your moods. Quick, what are you thinking about?"

"Corrie."

"Corrie? Oh, yeah. Gee, Sebastian, don't you think we should warn her? Why didn't you tell her about the shirt? I don't think she even noticed."

"She likes these people, David. I didn't want her thinking one of them is a murderer."

"And what if one of them *is* a murderer?"

"I don't know. I guess I should tell her, but—"

"But?"

"We could be wrong."

"Yeah, and we could be right."

Sebastian nodded. "I know, I know." He thought for a moment. "Corrie's home now, right? She's safe. And Alex and Rebecca will be over there in the morning while we're at school. And anyway, there are always other people around. So nothing will happen to her. Listen, speaking of school, I've got homework to finish and it's after nine. I put my stuff in your basket. Is your bike out back?"

"Yeah. My stuff's there, too. I'll go down with you."

Rachel and Josh were putting away the board game as the boys passed through the kitchen moments later. "Are you going to marry Rebecca?" they heard Rachel ask her father. "She's not planning to wear her uniform at the wedding, is she? Will I have to call her Lieutenant Mommy?"

They didn't wait to hear Josh's answer, if there was one.

The backyard was all silver and white in the light of a full moon. The boys made out their bicycles leaning against the side of the garage. When Sebastian lifted out his books, he found one that was not his.

"Look what we forgot," he said. Taking care not to rip the pages, he opened the book David had unearthed near the creek. The light was not sufficient to make out the words, but it was immediately apparent what it was.

"A Bible," David said. Then, squinting, he asked, "What's all this?"

Sebastian raised the book until the light of the

moon made the white pages glow. The margins were filled with a tiny script as indecipherable and as full of mystery as hieroglyphics discovered on the walls of an ancient tomb.

25

"I oughta put you fellas on the payroll," said Alex Theopoulos. It was 7:48 Tuesday morning; the police station thermometer registered thirty-one degrees outside, eighty-five in. Alex reached into his pocket for a handkerchief to wipe away the sweat about to drip into his eyes. "Sauna," he mumbled as he perused the small book the boys had just handed him. "It's like a sauna in here."

"What do you think all the writing means?" Sebastian asked. "It's not English."

"It's not any language I ever saw," said Alex. "Not that I'm a linguist, mind you. There's something very peculiar about it, though, sort of . . . unreal, spacey."

"Maybe an alien dropped it out of his UFO," David said, only half joking.

Alex flipped through the book. "There's writing everywhere," he observed, "though more on some pages than others. Look at this part here. You can hardly make out the text there's so much scribbling."

Again, Sebastian asked, "What do you think it means?"

"Beats me," said Alex.

"Could I see it again?" David asked.

Alex gave the Bible to David and turned to Sebastian. "By the way," he said, "we've tracked down the owners of the inn. They're coming to town on Friday."

He blotted his forehead with the handkerchief. "Can you believe this? It's not even eight o'clock and my one and only handkerchief is sopping wet. This day's going to be a beaut."

Seeing that David was still absorbed in looking at the Bible, Sebastian asked, "Do you know yet who the guy was who was murdered?"

Alex nodded. "He had some positive ID on him. I can't tell you because we're still trying to find next of kin. I'll tell you one thing, though. It's a pity. He was a young man, only twenty-six. We don't have the coroner's report yet, but at a glance I'd say he'd been through some hard living in his few years. Sebastian, my friend, there are times I would gladly trade my job for any you can name. There's too much heartbreak in it."

David looked up. "Are you going to check out the other stuff we told Rebecca about? The shirt and the rock?"

Alex nodded. "Don't worry, my young detectives, we will follow through this morning. And just in case our culprit is in fact one of the people staying at the church, I've asked Rebecca to spend the day there. Out of uniform. We don't want any trouble."

Sebastian glanced up at the clock behind Alex's desk. "Is that the right time?" he asked.

"That clock is one of the few things that work around here."

"We're going to be late. Come on, David, let's get out of here. We'll see you later, Alex."

92

"I'll see you, boys. Thanks for your help." Alex took the Bible back from David. "So did you manage to decode this thing?" he asked.

"I wasn't trying," David said. "I was looking at these pages with all the scribbling to see if I could figure out which part of the Bible it was."

"And?"

"It's a section called the *akedah* in Hebrew. We studied it in religious school."

"What's that in English?"

"It means 'the binding.' But sometimes it's called something else."

"What's that?" Alex asked.

" 'The sacrifice,' " said David.

26

"I've been thinking," Sebastian said when he spotted his friend in the school corridor later that day. It was a few minutes to two, just before their last class was to begin.

"Do your teachers know you're engaged in a subversive activity during school hours?" David asked. He was fiddling with the combination to his locker. "It keeps sticking," he said. "If that Mikey Kaufman put Krazy Glue on it again . . ."

"I've been thinking about the Bible," said Sebastian.

"There's a glue-wielding maniac on the loose and you want to talk theology?"

"It's important, David. Pay attention, we don't have much time until the bell rings."

"Okay, okay, my eyes are on this lock. My ears are all yours."

Sebastian leaned against the locker next to David's and said, almost in a whisper, "I can't believe we overlooked it, it seems so obvious. If there was a lot more scribbling in that one section of the Bible, then it must mean something, right?"

David nodded absently.

"So tell me the story of the—what did you call it?"

"The *akedah*. Let me get this straight, Sebastian. We have ninety seconds until our next class, my locker is glued for life, my homework is trapped inside, and you want me to tell you a Bible story?"

"Are you listening to me? This could be really important!"

"You're right. As usual. Here, you try the lock, I'll tell the story."

The boys changed places. "Okay," David began, "the *akedah*. There is this old guy, see, who God puts to the test. He tells him, 'Take your favorite son and sacrifice him.' See, in those days, people sacrificed animals as part of their religion. So this old guy, he never questions God, he just takes his son and they go up on this mountain and they gather all this wood for a burnt offering, and the son says, 'Where's the sheep we're going to sacrifice?' And the father doesn't know what to say, so he just tells him God will provide the sheep. So they put all the wood down for a fire and the father lays his son down on the wood and pulls out a knife, and he's just about ready to slay the son when an angel of the Lord appears and says, 'Hold it! You've proven that you love God, you don't have to sacrifice your son.' And just then a sheep appears and the old man sacrifices it instead."

There was a loud click followed by an even louder clanging of bells. "Your locker is open," said Sebastian.

"Yeah, and I'm going to be late. So, Sherlock, what do you make of the story?" David knelt down to rummage through a mess of papers on the floor of his locker.

"I don't know. It's an *almost* murder. What were their names, the father and son?"

"Abraham and Isaac," said David. His hand stopped moving, and he looked up at Sebastian.

"Abraham and Isaac," he repeated. "I can't believe I didn't make the connection before. The guy at the church is named Abraham."

Sebastian knelt down by David's side. "Remember what Corrie told us?" he said in an excited whisper. "She asked him if he had any family, and he said something about Isaac."

"Wow."

"How old would you say Abraham is?"

"At the time of the *akedah?* A hundred and thirty-seven, I think."

"Not the one in the Bible, the one at the church. He's old, too, right? Maybe forty or fifty?"

David nodded. "And the guy who was killed was twenty-six. Holy cow, Sebastian, you're not saying this guy murdered his own son, are you?"

"I don't know, but we've got to tell Alex."

"Not now."

"I know not now. It'll have to wait until after school."

"I've got music practice."

"I'll go alone then."

"Speaking of going—"

"Yeah, I'm late, too. Did you find your homework?" Sebastian asked as the boys stood and David slammed his locker shut.

"I, uh, had it in my notebook the whole time. But don't feel bad. I needed my oboe anyway. I'll see you later."

Sebastian looked across the hall. Miss Gerrard was already at the blackboard. "And speaking of murder," he said, more to himself than David. Miss Gerrard was not one to excuse latenesses. He was in for it.

27

Miss Gerrard tapped the board with her pointer.

"Sebastian Barth," she said, "this is the third time I have asked you to pay attention. Are you ill?"

Sebastian shook his head and ignored the sound of his classmates' snickering. "I'm fine," he said.

"Your definition of 'fine' and mine are not likely to be found in the same dictionary. One more warning and I will have to ask you to stay after school. Now, if we may continue our review, please explain to us the function of the electoral college."

Sebastian heard himself talking but his mind had narrowed in on one word Miss Gerrard had uttered: warning.

Corrie sat three seats ahead of him and one row over. He had to let her know that Abraham was not as harmless as he seemed, to urge her not to go to the church after school. Afraid she would be surrounded by a group of friends the moment class let out, he decided to pass her a note as soon as Miss Gerrard's attention was elsewhere.

"Thank you, Mr. Barth," he heard the teacher say. "An intelligent—if distracted—dissertation. Milo Groot, how did the two-party system evolve in American politics?"

Milo sat on the far side of the room in the front

seat of the row next to the windows. He was always good for a five-minute answer to a one-minute question. Now was the time.

Carefully, silently, Sebastian opened his notebook and tore out a blank sheet of paper. On it he wrote: *Corrie, Meet me after class—in private. It's important! S.*

He folded the sheet of paper and wrote Corrie's name on the outside. "Pass it on," he whispered to Adam Wells as he tapped him on the shoulder.

"Is it a love note?" Adam whispered back.

Sebastian made a face and poked him hard. "Do it," he hissed. Miss Gerrard looked up just as both boys looked down.

"What *is* it, Mr. Barth?" she said.

"I didn't say anything," Sebastian lied.

The teacher shook her head. "My patience is like the seat of a bus driver's pants," she said. "Worn thin."

"Yes, Miss Gerrard."

"Continue, Milo. You were saying . . ."

Sebastian followed the note's journey as it made its way down the row of seats in front of him. With each movement, he darted a glance across the room.

Janis Tupper leaned across the aisle separating her seat from Corrie's. "Psst," she said.

"I'll take that, Janis," said Miss Gerrard, walking briskly across the front of the room and snatching the piece of paper up with such abruptness it actually snapped.

"I'm afraid Corrie will be unable to keep your date, Sebastian," the teacher said, after making a show of opening and reading the note. "You already have a date. With me."

"But," said Sebastian, knowing he had nothing to say after "but," but hoping against hope that offering that much would imply he had an important reason for doing what he did.

"But you have a date with me," said Miss Gerrard. "And I assure you, we won't be having ice cream sundaes."

The class laughed openly at this. Sebastian hated them all for betraying him over a one-liner—and not a very clever one at that.

When the bell rang fifteen minutes later, Sebastian jumped up, hoping to reach Corrie before Miss Gerrard could stop him.

"Sit," said the teacher.

"I have to tell Corrie something," he said. "It's important, Miss Gerrard. Honest. It's a matter of life and death."

Miss Gerrard smirked. "At your age," she said, "pimples are a matter of life and death. You and Corrie can discuss blackheads on your own time. Right now, you're still on my time. And on my time, you are going to write an essay on the First Amendment."

"Isn't that the right to free speech?" Sebastian asked.

"Precisely," said the teacher, missing the irony.

"Find David," Sebastian mouthed to Corrie as he collapsed into his seat.

"What?" she mouthed back.

"Find David," he repeated.

Corrie just shrugged. "I don't understand," her

face told him. Before he could try again, Sebastian heard Miss Gerrard say, "Goodbye, Corrie Wingate." And Corrie, looking apologetic, stepped out and disappeared into the crowded hall.

28

"Wait up!" David shouted.

Sebastian turned and saw his friend running down the hall toward him, his oboe case banging against his thigh.

"I thought I saw you go by the music room a minute ago," David said, catching his breath. "What are you doing here? Did you tell Alex? What did he say? Why'd you come back to school?"

"To answer your last question first, I never left. Geronimo caught me passing a note to Corrie and made me stay after. I just got sprung."

"You mean Alex doesn't know?"

"Not unless he figured it out for himself." Hearing his own words, Sebastian laughed. "Gee, I never thought of that," he said. "Maybe the police have this case solved by now—*without* us."

"Well," said David, "there's one way to find out."

"Right," Sebastian said, zipping his jacket and shoving the school door open with his shoulder. "Next stop, the Pembroke Sauna."

"The chief isn't here," the sergeant at the front desk said briskly. He waited to add, "He's out on a call."

David turned to leave, but Sebastian asked, "Is he at the church?"

"I'm not at liberty to say," the sergeant answered. He was a small man with thin lips who seemed to take pleasure in hoarding what he viewed as privileged information.

Sebastian persevered. "It's important that we find him," he said.

The sergeant sighed. "Do you want to fill out a report?" he asked, opening a desk drawer. "What is it—your bike was stolen?"

"Nobody's bike was stolen," Sebastian replied. "We wouldn't waste the chief's time with something like that."

"So what is it? You can tell me."

"That's okay. We'll tell Alex when we find him. Thanks for all your help."

The sergeant gave the boys an open-handed shrug, as if to say, "What can I do? I tried."

"What a jerk," David said outside.

"Yeah, and we're a couple of jerks, too," said Sebastian. "Here we are trying to find Alex when we know Rebecca is at the church. Let's go tell her."

"Do you think Corrie will be there?"

"Probably."

"Corrie and the killer," said David. "Hey, that's a good title."

"This isn't the time for creative writing," Sebastian said, grabbing David's arm and breaking into a run. "It's time to move fast."

Rebecca was waiting in the church vestibule.

"Alex is on his way over," she told the boys. "He's

getting an okay from the assistant DA to issue an arrest warrant."

"You talked to him?" Sebastian asked.

"Does that surprise you?"

"When, just now?"

"A few minutes ago."

"He was at the station?"

Rebecca nodded. "Why?"

Sebastian exchanged a look of disgust with David. "Never mind," he said. "We'll tell you later."

"Wow," said David, "an arrest warrant. And to think we broke the case. The rock, the shirt, the Bible—"

"Is Corrie downstairs?" Sebastian asked.

"Yes. She's with her father."

"Can we go down?"

"I'll go with you," Rebecca said. "There's really no reason I need to wait here for Alex."

Descending the stairs to the basement social hall, Rebecca said, "So you figured out who did it."

It sounded to Sebastian as if they were playing a game of Clue all of a sudden instead of talking about a real live murder case.

"It's obvious, isn't it?" he said as they opened the door at the bottom of the stairs. As he looked around, the obvious no longer seemed so.

Across the room, Abraham sat listening to Corrie play her guitar. He was leaning against the wall, his eyes closed, one hand raised in the air, the index finger just touching his slightly open mouth. He looked at peace and as innocent as a sleeping child.

In another part of the room, Raymond Elveri was talking to the Reverend Wingate. In his hands he held a Bible.

Estelle Barker was reading to her children from a book Sebastian recognized from when he was little. But the words were all wrong. It dawned on him that she was making up a story to go with the pictures. Estelle Barker couldn't read. That meant, Sebastian thought, that she couldn't write either. Was it her hand that had covered the Bible David had found with that peculiar script?

David poked him. Sebastian nodded. "I know," his eyes said, "she's wearing the shirt."

Marcus was lying on his cot, staring at the ceiling. He wasn't reading, but he had been. Next to him was the detective magazine Sebastian had discovered at the inn.

No one had looked up when they'd quietly entered the room. But when the door opened again, this time with greater force and preceded by the sound of heavy footsteps rushing down the stairs, everyone turned.

Police Chief Alex Theopoulos stood in the doorway, a somber expression on his face and a piece of paper in his left hand.

It was not his left hand Sebastian noticed first, however. It was the right hand, resting lightly on the handle of the gun.

29

"Reverend Wingate, may I have a word?"

Corrie's father was clearly disturbed but not surprised by the appearance of the police chief. Sebastian figured that Rebecca must have tipped him off.
The minister crossed the room as Corrie stopped her
playing.

Sebastian was close enough to hear Alex whisper,
"If you would ask the children and Mrs. . . ."

"Barker."

"Yes, if you would ask them to leave with you,
please." Seeing the look on the minister's face, he
added, "I'm sorry to have to do this. It's unpleasant,
I know."

Reverend Wingate shook his head. "It's not a matter of its being unpleasant," he said. "I just feel so
sorry for—" He stopped abruptly, leaving Sebastian
to wonder *whom* he felt sorry for, and in a normal
voice said, "Corrie, would you come with me, please?
Mrs. Barker, would you bring Alyssa and Devon
along?"

Estelle Barker opened her mouth to object, but the
minister's raised hand warded off any argument, and
so she rose, speechless, and held out her own hands
to her children. Corrie was not so quick to acquiesce.

"What's going on?" she asked.

105

"I'll explain outside," her father said. "I think it would be best if you came with me."

Corrie looked from Raymond to Marcus to Abraham. Each had the wide-eyed look of someone guilty who had been found out at last. She didn't understand what was going on, but she wanted to protect them, each of them, even if they were guilty of something.

"I'm not going anywhere until you tell me what's happening," she said.

"Corrie—"

Alex touched Junior's arm. "Corrie"—Alex's voice deepened to an authoritative baritone—"this is a police matter. I must ask you to leave at once."

Corrie hesitated, then turned to Abraham. "Will you watch my guitar?" He didn't answer. He didn't even look at her as she got up from the cot. As she walked away, she thought what a dumb thing it was to have said. Nothing was going to happen to her guitar. It was Abraham who needed watching.

From her father's office she heard him being led away. He was howling, all gibberish and senseless rage. And then, as her father held her and she tried, unsuccessfully, to hold back her tears, she heard him cry out:

"I am Isaac! I am Abraham! I am Isaac!"

30

Corrie accepted an invitation to David's house for dinner that night. She didn't really want to go, but she didn't want to be home either. She told Sebastian she didn't know what she wanted, except for this day never to have happened.

Now she sat, her plate barely touched, half-listening to Rachel prattle on about her new exercise regimen.

"See, it's like a cross between Jane Fonda and Richard Simmons," she said, crunching a raw carrot.

"I shudder to think," said Josh. "Mouth closed, please."

Rachel continued through clenched teeth, chewing like a rabbit. "Me and my friend Lindsay—"

Josh said, "My friend Lindsay and I."

"Daddy!"

"Okay, okay."

"Me and my friend Lindsay put it together. See, we have these charts we made and . . ."

Corrie closed her eyes. She tried to imagine where Abraham was now; she saw him in handcuffs, in a cell, alone. Her throat burned as if it had been rubbed raw with sandpaper. She wondered how the others could swallow.

Sebastian bumped her knee with his. Opening her eyes, she tried, in vain, to smile. Josh caught the exchange and said, "Rachel, I think we've heard enough about you and your friend Jane."

"Lindsay."

"Whatever. Let's give somebody else a chance to talk, okay?"

"How's your book going?" Sebastian asked, latching onto the first thing that came to mind.

Josh brightened. "Great!" he said. "Sebastian, since I got this idea, I'm a new man. The writing is just pouring out of me. Today I wrote a scene where a body is found in a window seat—okay, so I stole it from a play I saw once—but I'm telling you, it had me in tears, it was so funny."

"How can you?" Corrie muttered.

Josh looked up, startled. "Sorry?" he said. "Oh, maybe we should talk about something else."

"It's not talking about it that I mean," Corrie said, keeping her eyes on her plate even as her voice rose. "It's your writing it. There's nothing funny about murder."

"Not *real* murder, no."

"Not *any* murder." She dared to raise her eyes and use them to accuse Josh. "Murder is the taking of life," she said. "How can you make that funny? People dying, people . . . people hurting so much they kill somebody, how can you turn that into . . . entertainment? That man was killed at the inn, Josh, *really* killed, and they're saying maybe Abraham did it, even though he didn't, I *know* he didn't; and you take what really happened and you call it an *idea* and give it a funny title and make money from it. From other people's pain." Her voice was shaking

108

now. "I don't know how you can do that, Josh. *'Dew Drop Dead.'* Someone *did* drop dead, and it isn't funny!"

She looked down at her plate again. The sight of the cold food turned her stomach, so she closed her eyes and breathed in slowly, counting the way she did when she ran. The room fell silent, except for the ticking of the clock. It made her think of the grandfather clock in the hallway of the inn and she bit into her lip so hard she wondered if she'd made it bleed.

"Corrie," Josh said, "maybe this isn't the best time for this conversation. I know you're feeling bad about what happened. And it *is* a tragedy. But I'm not going to apologize for what I do. I want you to know that I don't confuse real suffering with the stuff that's found in books and movies. Nothing I can write—I don't care if it moves you to tears or makes you want to change the world—nothing can compare with one moment of real pain. Or real joy, for that matter. Look, all I want to do is tell a good story. I wouldn't mind if I gave my readers a good laugh or a cry along the way. Maybe I'll even get them to think a little. And if they look at *real* life differently—the pain they see in others, the pain they feel themselves—that's about the best I can hope for."

"But why make it funny?" Corrie asked.

"Because people need to laugh. We're all afraid of the dark, Corrie. We're like David here—when we're the most afraid, we most need to giggle."

"I guess," Corrie said. "I just don't feel much like laughing now. You know?"

Josh nodded. "I know," he said.

The doorbell rang.

"I'll get it," David said, shoving Rachel back into her chair.

A moment later, he returned with Alex and Rebecca in tow.

"Just stopped by to say hello," Alex said. Seeing Sebastian and Corrie, he asked, "How are you two doing tonight? Corrie?"

"Okay," Corrie mumbled.

"Join us for dessert?" Josh asked. "Rachel, help your brother clear the table."

"But—"

"It's good exercise. Jane Fonda recommends it."

"Of course we'll join you for dessert," said Alex, tossing his hat on a pile of newspapers on the counter. "You don't think the timing of this visit is accidental, do you?"

Alex pulled up a couple of chairs for himself and Rebecca.

"So can you tell us what really happened?" David asked, once the dirty dinner plates had been replaced by clean ones and dessert was being passed around.

"As much as we know," said Alex. "We've just sent the shirt to forensics, along with Abraham's shoes to see if they match the footprints out by the creek. And we're still waiting on the coroner's report. Admittedly, the evidence we have is largely circumstantial."

"You mean Abraham might be innocent?" Corrie asked.

"He is innocent," Alex said.

Corrie looked confused. "But you arrested him."

"He's innocent until proven guilty. We arrested
110

him because we suspect he committed the crime. Since he's an unknown and homeless, we can't risk his running out on us. But I'm getting ahead of myself."

"The dead man was named Kevin Moore," said Rebecca.

"Not Isaac?" Sebastian asked, surprised.

Alex shook his head. "From his identification, we were able to locate his mother in a trailer park in Pennsylvania. She said her son had called her about a week ago to let her know where he was. He told her he was traveling with a man named Abraham, whom he described as being 'crazy but kind.'"

"She also told us," said Rebecca, picking up the story, "that her son had a long history of problems, including alcohol abuse. He'd started running away from home when he was twelve. But he always called her to let her know where he was."

"So she wouldn't worry," Alex said, shaking his head. "What did she call him? 'A good boy living a bad life.' Anyway, as she described it, this man, Abraham, had become a sort of father figure to Kevin, and she was glad to know someone was watching out for him."

"Then why would Abraham kill him?" Corrie said. "It doesn't make sense."

"Who knows?" said Alex. "We're a long way from having the answer to that. All we know is that the deceased was traveling with a man named Abraham, that the man named Abraham at the church was in possession of the magazine and shirt you said you saw at the inn—yes, he admitted they were his, along with the Bible you found by the creek. And— Rebecca, why don't you show them the picture?"

Rebecca leaned back in her chair and reached for the bag lying next to Alex's hat on the counter. "By the way," she said, "your pie is out of this world. Don't tell me you made it, Josh. I don't know if I can stand it. You're too perfect."

Josh placed a hand over each of his kids' mouths. "That's what Rachel and David tell me all the time," he said.

The deputy lifted a framed photograph out of her bag and laid it on the table. "Is this the one you said was missing from the inn?" she asked.

Sebastian nodded. "Where'd you find it?"

"Among Abraham's belongings. He kept it under the mattress of his cot at the church."

Corrie lifted it slowly, wondering again who the people were. Aloud, she said, "Happy times."

Alex broke the silence that followed by telling David, "Your pointing out that section of the Bible helped us put it all together, you know."

"It did?" David asked, unable to help looking pleased with himself.

"Abraham and Isaac. It seems to be a fixation with the man. We don't know if Abraham is his real name. I doubt it. We've fingerprinted him, and I wouldn't be surprised if he's been printed before. We should have an ID soon. He's ill, that much is certain. And it's not uncommon for seriously disturbed people to have religious delusions. Perhaps he thought he *was* the biblical Abraham. Perhaps he believed he was meant to sacrifice Isaac, the man he thought of as Isaac."

Corrie touched the photograph, the place where the name was written on the side of the boat, and said, "I think I'd like to go home now."

Sebastian rose with her. "I'll walk with you," he said.

They walked wordlessly through the cold night air until they reached Corrie's house. Standing at her door, all they could think to say was, "See you tomorrow."

31

Sebastian opened the front door of his own house a few minutes later. His mother called out, "Is that you, Will? I'm in the kitchen."

"Just me," Sebastian said, poking his head around the kitchen door. Katie had what looked like every pot and pan they owned going at once.

"Oh, hello, dear. I thought it might be your father. He said he'd be home early tonight."

Sebastian glanced at his watch. "Quarter to nine is early?" he asked. "What are you making, anyway? Smells good."

"I'm trying out variations of potato-and-leek soup for the restaurant. Want some?"

He shook his head and pulled out a chair to sit. Boo woke to the sound of the chair leg scraping across the linoleum and roused himself sufficiently to meander over, jump up on Sebastian's lap, and fall back to sleep. "How come Dad's working so late these days?" Sebastian asked.

"Three reasons," Katie answered. "Meetings, meetings, and more meetings." She raised a spoon to her lips and tasted. "Needs something. What?"

Without thinking, Sebastian said, "Pimento. Just don't borrow it from Josh."

"What? Oh, pimento, what a good idea. Thank you, dear."

"Where's Gram?"

"Upstairs. She's on long-distance with Aunt Rose. Sebastian—"

"No."

"No what?"

"I don't want to talk to Aunt Rose."

"I wasn't going to ask you to. For heaven's sake. I just wanted to say ..." She stopped and took a breath, as if shifting gears. Sebastian looked up. "I just wanted to say that your father and I are sorry for all the tension around here lately. You haven't said a word, but I know it hasn't been easy for you."

"It's okay."

"No, it's not okay." Katie turned to stir the soup as she continued speaking. "Your dad and I grew up in Pembroke, Sebastian. We moved back here after college because we couldn't imagine a better place to live. Our friends are here, our work is here, our lives are here. The last thing we want is to have to move. But we may have no choice unless ... well, it looks almost certain your dad's going to lose his job."

It took Sebastian a moment to speak. "Where would we go?" he asked.

Katie sighed. "I don't know. Your father is looking into other stations in Connecticut. But there aren't that many openings right now."

"What if he can't find anything?" Sebastian said. Boo began to purr contentedly, obliviously, under his master's hand.

"We have savings and there *is* the income from the restaurant, although it isn't much. We'd get by."

115

Katie took another taste of soup and added, "For a while, anyway." She laughed lamely.

"What's so funny?" Sebastian asked.

"Nothing. I was just thinking how it wasn't very long ago that our lives seemed perfect."

Sebastian didn't know what to say to this. He watched as Katie went back to her cooking. "How was your evening?" she asked. "Okay," he said. "What did Josh make?" "Pot roast." "You finished your homework?" "Before dinner." Their words didn't matter to either of them and even though it happened while they talked, it wasn't their words that made his mother start to cry.

"Aw, Mom," said Sebastian.

"Are you sure you don't want some soup?" Katie asked. "Come on." She pulled a bowl from a cabinet. "How can you refuse soup made with a mother's tears?"

Sebastian grimaced. "As David says, 'Oy vay.' "

This got Katie laughing. "Sebastian," she said, "I don't make promises I can't keep, but I will promise you this. There will be happier times ahead."

Her words made him think of Corrie. And of Abraham. And of the man who had died young at the Dew Drop Inn.

32

The next day after school, Sebastian and David rode their bikes out to radio station WEB-FM.

Denise, the receptionist, looked up from her knitting and greeted them with a warm hello. "Well, well, well, do my eyes deceive me?" she said. "Or is this not Sebastian Barth, famous detective and former talk show host, and his faithful companion and writer, David Lepinsky?"

"Gee, thanks, Denise," David said. "At least you didn't call me Tonto."

"Who's Tonto?"

"The Lone Ranger's sidekick. I thought you'd know that."

Denise pursed her lips. "Before my time, dear heart. Now what can I do you for?"

"We just dropped by to see my dad," Sebastian said. He looked around at the faded furniture in the waiting area. Before, when this place had been his second home, the sofas and chairs had seemed comfortable; now all they looked was shabby.

"You getting fired too, Denise?" David asked.

Denise's laughter rippled through the room like a breeze through an open window. "Honey," she said, "you are too much. No one is getting fired that I know of." She leaned across her desk and was about to whisper something when the door opened and Harry Dobbs appeared.

"Boys!" he shouted. "Where have you been keeping yourselves?" He threw his arms open wide as if Sebastian and David were a couple of toddlers he was waiting to gobble up. He had known both boys most of their lives and loved them as if they were his own flesh and blood, which, since he had no real family of his own, they may as well have been. They were so fond of him they called him Uncle Harry, even though he was old enough to be their grandfather. Sebastian had worried for a long time that Harry's days at the station were numbered. With all that had been going on of late, he was pretty sure the numbers were fast approaching zero.

"Hi, Uncle Harry," he said. "How are you doing?"

"As well as can be expected," said Harry, his arms still airborne, as if he'd forgotten where he'd put them, "considering that even as we speak one can hear the executioner's ax being sharpened in the adjacent chamber."

"That's the copy machine," said Denise.

Harry roared with laughter. "Ah, Denise," he cried, "if I were only blessed with your practical view of the world. As long as the copy machine keeps running, we're in business, eh?"

Annoyed, Denise shrugged. "Why not?" she said. "At least I have a reason to get up in the morning. And I don't pack my lunch in a bottle, like some people I could name. If you get my drift."

Harry kept laughing, but the sound of it had changed.

"We'll see you later, Uncle Harry," Sebastian

said, eager to escape. "We, uh . . . we wanted to say hi to Dad."

"Right you are," said Harry Dobbs, looking as worn as the furniture. "You know where to find him—down the hall, one door past the sound of the executioner's ax."

"Is Uncle Harry drinking again?" Sebastian asked his father as David closed the door behind them.

"Again?" said Will Barth. "When did he stop?"

David shook his head sadly. "What'll happen to him if he's fired?"

"That's a question I've asked myself repeatedly," Will said, looking off. "When I haven't been busy asking what's going to happen to me, that is." He turned his eyes to the boys and brought them into focus. "What's up?"

"Nothing," Sebastian said, trying to appear nonchalant. "I haven't seen you a whole lot lately, that's all."

"I know. And I'm sorry about that, I really am. But I think the worst is over. You'll see, things will get better soon."

"That's what Mom says."

Will smiled. "At least we agree on something," he said. Then, catching the look of discomfort on David's face, he quickly changed the subject. "Where's Corrie?"

Sebastian picked up a crystal paperweight from his father's desk. "Football practice," he answered, recognizing the object as an industry award Will had received a couple of months earlier.

"Is she doing all right? I spoke to her father this morning. He's pretty shook up to think he was harboring a murderer at the church. And who can blame him? Alex says the evidence is really stacked against this guy. He may get off on insanity, though."

"Corrie doesn't think Abraham's guilty," David said.

"No?"

Holding the paperweight, Sebastian studied the words: FOR EXCELLENCE IN BROADCASTING. "She says there's no way Abraham could kill anybody," he told his father. "She says he wouldn't even hurt a fly."

"And I say she's nuts," David said. "I mean, did you ever see this guy when he starts talking crazy? Whoa, let me outa here. He did it, all right. Corrie's just gone soft, that's all."

"Well," Will said, "maybe she got a little too involved. Not that I blame her. She's all heart, and more power to her for that. But when your heart gets in the way, your eyes don't always see clearly."

Sebastian said, "I get the feeling that she thinks if she says something enough times, it'll come true."

"What's she been saying?"

" 'He didn't do it.' " Running his fingers over the engraving on the paperweight, Sebastian said, "Every time I saw her in school today, that's all she could say. 'He didn't do it, Sebastian. I'm telling you, he didn't do it, he didn't do it.' "

"And what do you think?" Will asked.

"I'm not sure what to think anymore," said Sebastian, putting the paperweight back in its place on his father's desk.

33

"He didn't do it."

The words were not Corrie's this time, but Alex's.
Corrie, who had convinced Sebastian to drop by the
police station Friday afternoon after school in the
hope of visiting Abraham, was so stunned to hear
what the chief had just told them she'd already forgotten her initial disappointment in learning Abraham wasn't being held there but in the county jail.

"What do you mean?" Sebastian asked, since Corrie appeared to have been rendered speechless. "Did
somebody else confess?"

Alex shook his head. "There was no murder," he
said.

"No murder? I don't get it. There was a body,
right?"

"Sit down, you two. Here, Sebastian, pull that
chair over." Corrie and Sebastian sat on two uncomfortable wooden chairs—purposely uncomfortable,
Sebastian imagined—and waited for Alex to begin.
First, he mopped his forehead with a new handkerchief. "I'm buying them by the dozen," he said half-
apologetically. "Okay, here's the story.

"The coroner did us a favor and rushed his report.
We got it this morning. Kevin Moore did not die of
a blow to the head."

"He didn't?" Sebastian said.

"Nope. He died of hypothermia. Translated, means he froze to death."

"Oh, no," Corrie whispered.

"It happens sometimes to people living out in the elements, though it's rare that it happens to someone so young. Thing is, Kevin was a heavy drinker. Alcohol alone lowers your body temperature. Combined with all this below-freezing weather we've been having and the fact that he wasn't in good health to begin with, well . . ."

"The poor man," said Corrie. Sebastian nodded, unable even to imagine what it would be like to freeze to death.

"But what about Abraham?" he asked. "Where was he?"

"In bed, I guess. Our theory is that Kevin was out when Abraham went to sleep that night. Kevin either came back intoxicated or drank himself unconscious once he was back at the inn. In either case, he fell asleep without protecting himself from the cold—and Abraham was already asleep, so he couldn't do anything about it. We talked to Abraham in order to piece together what happened the next day. Bear in mind we are dealing with a very confused individual. The best we can figure is this.

"When he woke up, he discovered his friend wasn't breathing. Not only did he not know what to do, he probably wasn't even clear about what had happened. At some point, he started to feel guilty; if he hadn't been sleeping, after all, his friend might still be alive. He was scared, immobilized. Then you showed up. Abraham heard you, hid somewhere—in a closet, maybe in a shadow."

Corrie shivered. "So we *weren't* alone," she said.

"Definitely not. Although I don't think he really saw you; there wasn't enough light. And anyway, he never seemed to recognize you at the church. Okay, so he knew the body had been found. Once you left, he did the first thing that came to his mind—he removed the body from the inn. While he was at it, he tore the sleeve of the shirt Kevin was wearing and then, between the inn and the woods, dropped the body so that it hit something. That's the blow to the head and that's—"

"The blood on David's rock," said Sebastian, finishing the sentence for him.

"Why didn't he just run away?" Corrie asked.

"Because Kevin was his friend. He felt he needed to protect him. Remember, I said he's a confused individual. Once he had Kevin hidden in the woods, he thought about it and realized he couldn't go back to the inn to live. He took Kevin's shirt—for warmth, for remembrance, who knows?—then gathered a few of his own belongings together and hit the road. The only thing he didn't take was his Bible, which must have fallen out of his pocket when he was hiding Kevin's body.

"Somewhere out there, your father found him. And he in turn found his way to the church. And there he made another friend, Corrie. You."

Corrie sat quietly for a minute, taking it all in. "Do you think they'd let me see him at the county jail? I'm sure my mom or dad would take me."

"He's not there."

"But you said—"

"I said he *was* there. He's no longer a suspect, Corrie. He had to be released."

123

Corrie said, "Where is he then?" But even as she asked the question, she knew the answer Alex would give.

"Somewhere out there."

34

A loud buzz jarred Corrie from her thoughts.

"Yes," Alex said into the box on his desk.

"A Mrs. Weatherall to see you, Chief." Sebastian recognized the obsequious voice on the other end as belonging to the small sergeant at the front desk.

"Thank you, Sergeant Macy. Ask her to come in." He turned to Sebastian and Corrie. "I'm sorry," he said, "you'll have to excuse me."

"Is it okay if we wait outside?" Sebastian asked. "We told David to meet us here."

"It's fine with me," Alex replied, rising in anticipation of his next appointment. "Just stay clear of Sergeant Macy. He doesn't hold kids in particularly high regard."

"I noticed," said Sebastian. There was a knock on the door. Alex opened it and a tall, nervous-looking woman, one hand still raised, was waiting on the other side.

"Mrs. Weatherall," Alex said, "please come in."

Corrie and Sebastian nodded to the stranger, whose eyes barely registered their presence, and went out into the main room.

They seated themselves on a long bench as far from Sergeant Macy as they could get. After a time, Corrie said, "My sister, Alice, says it's dumb to get involved in other people's lives. Maybe she's right, I don't know. She never gets hurt."

"I thought you said she cried all the time."

"Over boys. That's different. Alice goes through boys faster than she goes through fingernail polish. And you know what? It takes her polish longer to dry than her tears. No, I'm talking about real hurt."

"The kind you're feeling?"

Corrie nodded. "Remember the other day, before we went to the inn, David said we should just stay young forever? Maybe we should."

"Hey, listen," Sebastian said, "in the end, even Peter Pan got hurt, didn't he?"

They felt a cold rush of wind as the front door of the police station blew open and David hurried in. Sergeant Macy made noises about the draft, but no one paid attention. When David spotted his friends, he waved and ran over to them.

"Hey, guess what," Sebastian said. "Abraham's innocent."

"He's what?"

"He's even been set free," said Corrie. "There wasn't a murder, after all."

David pinched the back of his hand. "Have I been dreaming this whole thing?" he asked. "Didn't we see a body?"

Before Sebastian or Corrie could answer, Alex's door opened. "Good, I'm glad you're still here," he called across the room. "You want to come in for a minute?"

Sergeant Macy stood, picking up a notepad as he did. "Not you, Sergeant. I'm talking to my friends there."

126

"What friends?" the sergeant asked. "I just see a bunch of kids."

"Those are my friends. Come on, I want you to meet someone. I think you'll find this quite interesting."

The woman they had passed in Alex's doorway now sat on the chair Corrie had previously occupied. She looked calmer, although still clearly upset. When Alex saw that there weren't enough chairs, he called out to Sergeant Macy to bring in two more, winking slyly at the kids as he did so. It was easy to see whose side Alex was on.

When they were all seated, Alex said, "This is Catherine Weatherall. She and her husband are the owners of the Dew Drop Inn."

"More to the point," said the woman, "I am Bill Conroy's sister."

David and Corrie were puzzled, but Sebastian got it at once. "Bill Conroy is Abraham," he said.

"He called himself Abraham, yes. Bill is the reason my husband and I left the inn the way we did, why we disappeared without a trace."

"It sounds like you were running away from him," Corrie said.

"We were." The directness of the woman's response startled them.

"But why?" said Corrie. "Why didn't you help him?"

Catherine Weatherall drew her legs under her and folded her hands in her lap, reining in her body as if protecting it from the attack she anticipated. "Bill is a very sick man," she said. "And a very difficult one. He's been in and out of institutions all his adult life. Years ago, when it first became obvious he was

127

ill and my parents had him committed to a hospital, he started blaming them for all his troubles. As soon as he was released, he unleashed all his anger on them, hounding them night and day, making their lives miserable. I was away at college then, so I escaped what was an unendurably painful time for my parents.

"A little over five years ago, my mother died. Soon after, my father met a French woman on a cruise and with remarkable haste, married her. Imagine, he didn't speak a word of French, but he didn't hesitate to pick up and move to a small village in France. It was, for him, a new life. Or a chance at one, at least. I was furious with him at the time. Now I understand. And I don't blame him at all.

"Without my parents around, Bill turned his anger on me. We had been very, very close as children. I loved him dearly. But he was not the same Bill I had known as a child. And clearly he didn't see me as the same Catherine, either. He began calling me Catherine the Second. By his logic the first Catherine—the one who had loved him, the one who had been kind to him as a child—was dead. I was someone else, Catherine in name only. Catherine the Second. He took to calling himself Isaac some time later."

"Why Isaac?" Sebastian asked. "And where did Abraham come from?"

"In the Bible, Isaac was the son betrayed by his father. Bill saw himself as betrayed by his family. I don't know why he took to calling himself Abraham later on. He had his reasons, I'm sure."

"He called me Catherine the First," said Corrie.

"Probably because you reminded him of me when

I was your age." Catherine Weatherall took some-thing from Alex's desk and handed it to Corrie. It was the photograph, now removed from its frame. "Look. Look what it says on the back."

" 'With Catherine and Bill on the Cape, summer 195?. *Happy Times* freshly painted.' " Corrie turned the picture over. "So this is his family, his real fam-ily. I still don't understand how you could all run away and leave him. He's your brother."

"I have children, Corrie, a boy and a girl. He tried to turn them against me and when that didn't work, took to spying on them and shouting obscenities at them. What could I do? I had to protect them and I had to protect myself. We moved, and he followed us. We moved again, and he followed us again. We bought the inn during one of Bill's hospitalizations a few years ago. We thought our moving days were over. But somehow he found us, and it started again, all the unhappiness. Finally, we had no choice but to vanish."

There was a long silence as Corrie studied the photograph. "I was just thinking," she said. "The people in this picture look so nice."

She handed it back and Catherine said, "Do you want to keep it? It makes me too sad."

Corrie shook her head. "It makes me sad, too," she said.

"Please don't hate me, Corrie. What I've done is harder than you can possibly imagine. It's a terrible thing to have to choose between your brother and yourself. But that's the choice I had to make."

"What will happen to the picture if neither of us takes it?"

"I suppose it will be thrown away," said Catherine Weatherall.

"I'll keep it then," Corrie said. "I'll save it."

"For Abraham?" The woman knew which name to use.

"Yes," said Corrie. "I'm sure he misses it. Maybe I'll see him again someday and I can give it back to him."

The woman nodded.

"I mean," Corrie said, "it's the only family he's got left."

35

Later that afternoon, Sebastian was lying on his bed reading when a piece of fallen paper caught his eye.

"Dear Koji," he read, picking it up. *"How's everything with you? I'm having a pretty good year in school. Mom and Dad are fine. Gram is busy with all her projects, as usual. There's not much happening here."*

It seemed like a million years ago that he'd started this letter to his pen pal. What a letter he could write now! Dear Koji, My friends and I found a body in an abandoned inn. We thought the guy had been murdered, but it turned out . . . it turned out . . .

Sebastian wondered how Josh's novel would turn out. His *Dew Drop Dead* would be so different from the real thing. He wondered if it would make him laugh.

Just then, he heard laughter coming from the kitchen. The sound surprised him, and his surprise made him realize how long it had been since there was any *real* laughter in the house.

He went down to the kitchen where he found his father helping his mother make dinner.

"What are you doing home?" Sebastian asked.

"Well, hello to you, too," said Will. Then, with a

131

nod to the clock on the wall, he added, "It *is* after six."

"Did you get fired?"

"Not exactly."

"What do you mean, not exactly?"

Will ran some water over a head of lettuce. "I was informed that a few changes will be made once the 'transition' is complete," he told his son.

"That doesn't sound so bad."

Katie laughed lightly. "It's all code, Sebastian," she said. "When you're told directly that a few changes are to be made, what it means is that *you* are one of the changes."

Sebastian looked back and forth between his parents. "I don't get it," he said. "You guys look happy. I heard you laughing."

"Well, don't make it sound like a disease," said his mother.

Will put the lettuce into a salad spinner and handed it to Sebastian while he started to chop some carrots. "We're relieved," he said. "We've been worried and scared and feeling sorry for ourselves for too long. And you know something? Now that we realize it's really going to happen, it's not so bad."

"In a way," said Katie, "it's like being given a chance to start over. We've been talking about all the things we could do with our lives."

"Like what?" Sebastian asked, getting worried.

His mother thought a minute. "Like living on a beach somewhere and making masks out of coconut shells to sell to the tourists."

"Get real," Sebastian said.

"Well," said his father as Jessica entered the room, "we *did* entertain the notion—"

"For about twenty minutes," Katie interjected.

"—of buying the Dew Drop Inn," Will went on. "We've had this dream of being innkeepers since we were in college and—"

Sebastian began vigorously turning the handle of the salad spinner. "And we wouldn't have to leave Pembroke!" he cried. "And Mom could keep her restaurant—or even move it to the inn—and Uncle Harry could come work for us and—"

"Oh, that man!" said Jessica, scowling. "I won't have *him* working at our inn."

Sebastian turned to his parents. "But where would you get the money?" he asked. "Doesn't an inn cost an awful lot?"

"My sister Rose can help," said Jessica, taking the salad spinner from Sebastian and placing the nearly dry lettuce leaves in a large bowl. "What does she need all her money for? She doesn't have any children and I doubt she's bought herself a new dress in the past ten years. She could become a part-owner."

"Would she have to come live with us?" Sebastian asked.

Jessica gave Sebastian a long look. "You've never liked Rose, have you? I don't understand that. She's terribly fond of you."

"It isn't that I don't like Aunt Rose," Sebastian said, "exactly. It's just, well, I don't know if I'd like her living at the inn with us."

"Well, for goodness' sake, if she's going to put up the money, she's certainly entitled to *live* there. Which is more than I can say for Harry Dobbs."

"But Uncle Harry will *work* at the inn. What will Aunt Rose do?"

Sebastian's parents burst into laughter. "Cut it out, you two," Will pleaded. "We're not buying the inn."

"We're not?" said Sebastian.

"Oh," Jessica said, "Rose will be so disappointed."

Katie urged the family to sit down to dinner. "I'll admit we did seriously consider the idea," she said. "Briefly. We even made a call. But the inn isn't for sale."

"It isn't?" Sebastian asked.

"No," said Will. "It seems that Corrie's father has convinced the county to buy the place and turn it into a permanent shelter for the homeless."

"That's great," Sebastian said. Out of the corner of his eye, he noticed his grandmother shaking her head. "So are you going to look for another inn to buy?"

Katie laughed. "Not at the moment," she said. "But you never know what the future will bring."

"Well," said Jessica. "One thing the future will bring—and soon—is Thanksgiving. If one may be allowed to change the subject, I have something of the utmost importance I wish to discuss." She waited to be sure she had everyone's rapt attention before continuing.

"This sounds serious," said Will. "What is it?"

"Pies!" Jessica exclaimed. "I have decided to make a different kind this year. Mince."

"Oh, Gram," said Sebastian. "I hate mince. And anyway, apple and pumpkin are tradition."

"Well, that's true. And tradition matters. But I love mince, and I never make it because no one else likes it."

"Then I think you should make it," said Katie.

"But what about tradition?" Sebastian protested.

"Perhaps," said Katie, "the time has come for new traditions."

"I'll drink to that," Will said, raising his glass of water. "Here's to traditions: the old and familiar . . . and the ones waiting to be made."

36

Jessica Hallem's pies—the apple, the pumpkin, and the mince—were three among many that Thanksgiving. For Sebastian's family, as for other families in Pembroke, carrying food from their homes in wicker baskets and old cookie tins to the long cloth-covered table in the center of the basement social hall at First Church marked the beginning of a new holiday tradition.

By the time all the food—the turkey and pot roast, the mashed potatoes and yam pies, the bread stuffing and bowls of cranberry mold—had found its place on the overcrowded serving table, more than eighty people filled the room.

Estelle Barker's daughter, Alyssa, eyed the bounty at a distance before daring to come up and touch the white cloth with one tiny finger. "I thought I was dreaming it," she said.

"You are," her mother told her. "Tomorrow it's peanut butter for you again." Then, seeing the look in her daughter's eyes, she softened. "That's okay, honey lamb. You just fill up on this dream today."

Estelle and her two children sat at a table with David and Rachel and Josh. When Rebecca Quinn joined them, Estelle cried, "Now I'm the one that's dreaming! Thanksgiving dinner with the police! You children mind your manners, hear, or you'll be eating tomorrow's dinner off tin plates!"

Sebastian and his family were seated at a table nearby. Uncle Harry asked Jessica politely if the chair next to hers was taken, and before she could think what to say, he took it. Harley and his sisters joined them. His father, Harley explained, had to work that day. "People need gas even on Thanksgiving," he said. "And my dad needs his job."

When Sebastian saw that there was one empty chair left at the table, he walked over to Marcus, who was sitting sullenly in a far corner of the room.

"What are you up to, man?" Marcus asked as Sebastian took him firmly by the arm and led him to the table.

"Nobody sits alone today," Sebastian said.

He looked over to where Corrie was sitting with her own and another family—a mother, father, and three children, who, Sebastian learned later, had been living out of their car for over two months. Corrie saw him pulling Marcus along and smiled at them both.

The Reverend Wingate ruffled his daughter's hair as he passed behind her, and Corrie smiled up at him, too. She was proud that he had done this, brought all these people together—people with homes of their own who had chosen to celebrate Thanksgiving in a church basement instead, people without homes who today might have some small reason to celebrate.

She smiled to herself to think of Raymond Elveri, whose note had been given to her just that morning by the church custodian. *"Dear Corrie,"* it read. *"I've gone home to my family. Maybe they'll give me an-*

*other chance. Maybe this time I will, too. Happy
Thanksgiving. Your friend, Raymond."*

The cold November wind rattled the windows, and
Corrie's smile faded. Abraham was out there somewhere. Perhaps near. Perhaps far away by now. It
had been over a week since she'd seen him last. She
thought of the photograph that she had tucked away
in the bottom drawer of her dresser. She would save
it for him in case he returned. In case she ever saw
him again.

And she heard her father say, "Let us bow our
heads and give thanks."